PENGUIN BOOKS

PIERCING

Renaissance man for the modern age, Ryu Murakami has played drums for a rock group, made movies, and hosted a TV talk show. His first novel, *Almost Transparent Blue*, written while he was still a student, was awarded Japan's most coveted literary prize and went on to sell over a million copies. His most recent novel to appear in English was *In the Miso Soup*, published in 2006.

Ralph McCarthy is the translator of *69* and *In the Miso Soup* by Ryu Murakami, and two collections of stories by Osamu Dazzai.

PIERCING

RYU MURAKAMI

Translated by Ralph McCarthy

PENGUIN BOOKS

PENGUIN BOOKS

Published by the Penguin Group
Penguin Group (USA) Inc., 375 Hudson Street, New York, New York 10014, U.S.A.
Penguin Group (Canada), 90 Eglinton Avenue East, Suite 700, Toronto, Ontario,
Canada M4P 2Y3 (a division of Pearson Penguin Canada Inc.)
Penguin Books Ltd, 80 Strand, London WC2R 0RL, England
Penguin Ireland, 25 St Stephen's Green, Dublin 2,
Ireland (a division of Penguin Books Ltd)
Penguin Group (Australia), 250 Camberwell Road, Camberwell, Victoria 3124,
Australia (a division of Pearson Australia Group Pty Ltd)
Penguin Books India Pvt Ltd, 11 Community Centre,
Panchsheel Park, New Delhi–110 017, India
Penguin Group (NZ), 67 Apollo Drive, Mairangi Bay, Auckland 1311, New Zealand
(a division of Pearson New Zealand Ltd)
Penguin Books (South Africa) (Pty) Ltd, 24 Sturdee Avenue,
Rosebank, Johannesburg 2196, South Africa

Penguin Books Ltd, Registered Offices:
80 Strand, London WC2R 0RL, England

First published in Japan by Gentosha 1994
First published in Great Britain by Bloomsbury Publishing 2007
Published in Penguin Books 2007

3   5   7   9   10   8   6   4   2

Copyright © Ryu Murakami, 2007
Translation copyright © Ralph McCarthy, 2007
All rights reserved

ISBN 07475-8220-3 (hc.)
ISBN 978-0-14-303863-4 (pbk.)
CIP data available

Printed in the United States of America

A SMALL LIVING CREATURE asleep in its crib. Like a laboratory animal in a cage, thought Kawashima Masayuki. He used the palm of his hand to shade the penlight so that it illuminated only the baby's form, leaving the rest of the bedroom in darkness. Leaning in closer, he silently mouthed the words *Fast asleep*. As Yoko's pregnancy had progressed and the fact that he was actually going to be a father began to sink in, he'd worried that the baby might have difficulty sleeping. Kawashima had suffered from insomnia since elementary school, and, after all, his blood would run in this child's veins. He'd heard it was normal for newborns to sleep virtually around the clock; in fact, he seemed to recall some child-rearing expert describing sleep as an infant's 'job'. What could be more tragic, then, than a baby insomniac?

He turned softly to check on Yoko in the double

bed behind him. Her regular breathing assured him she was still asleep.

Kawashima had been doing this every night lately, standing there gazing down at the baby while his wife slept. Ten nights in a row now, to be exact. It was well after midnight, and since Yoko rose early each morning to prepare for work, she wasn't likely to awaken. A wholesome and healthy twenty-nine-year-old cooking expert, Yoko was a stranger to things like insomnia. She'd quit her job with a major manufacturer of baked goods when they married and begun giving lessons to people from the neighbourhood, right here in their one-bedroom apartment. Yoko's bread and pastry classes proved astonishingly popular, and now she had dozens of students – from housewives and middle-school girls to elderly widowers and even middle-aged men. She taught classes almost every day, taking only two fixed holidays a month, and the entire apartment, including this bedroom, was permeated with the buttery smell that for Kawashima had come to symbolise happiness. Little Rie (the name suggested by Yoko's mother) was now four months old, and Yoko somehow managed to look after her and still maintain a full teaching schedule. Of course, it didn't hurt that most of her students were female and always eager to help out with the baby.

He switched off the penlight for a moment and examined the pale moonbeam that sliced through a gap between the curtains. The narrow strip of light reached to the middle of the crib, slashing across the baby's pink blanket and the pocket of Kawashima's corduroy slacks. As a little boy he'd often sat in his room, with the moon his only source of light, drawing pictures of a long, narrow road that vanished in the distance. Remembering those times, and taking care not to prick his finger, he lifted the ice pick from his pocket. He closed his right hand around the handle and gently drew back the baby's blanket with his left. This exposed her neck and upper chest, whiter and softer even than the bread Yoko baked. He switched the penlight back on and shone it upon her cheeks and neck. It seemed to him that the fragrance of fresh bread grew suddenly more pronounced, mixed with another scent he didn't recognise. He wasn't aware of the beads of perspiration on his forehead and temples until he saw one drip on to the baby's blanket. The panel heater against the wall had warmed the room somewhat, but it was far from hot in here. The tip of the ice-pick was quivering slightly. Another bead rolled down Kawashima's saturated eyebrow and into the corner of his eye.

That's sickening, he thought, and squeezed his eyes

shut. Didn't even know I was sweating. Couldn't even feel it. Like it isn't me the sweat's pouring down but a wax figure of me, or some stranger who looks just like me. Damn.

As he opened his eyes he found that his senses of sight and sound and smell were getting entangled with one another, and now came a snapping, crackling sensation and a pungent whiff of something organic burning. Yarn or fingernails, something like that.

He moaned beneath his breath: *Not again.*

It always started with the sweating, followed by this smell of charred tissue. Then a sudden sense of utter exhaustion, and finally that indescribable pain. As if the particles of air were turning to needles and piercing him all over. A prickling pain that spread like goose bumps over his skin until he wanted to scream. Sometimes a white mist clouded his vision and he could actually see the air particles turning into needles.

Calm down, he told himself. Relax, you're all right, you've already made up your mind you'll never stab her. Everything's going to be all right.

Gripping the ice pick lightly to minimise trembling, he placed the point of it next to the baby's cheek. Every time he studied this instrument, with its slender, gleaming steel rod that tapered down to

4

such needle-like sharpness, he wondered why it was necessary to have things like this in the world. If it were truly only for chopping ice, you'd think a completely different design might do. The people who produce and sell things like this don't understand, he thought. They don't realise that some of us break out in a cold sweat at just a glimpse of that shiny, pointed tip.

The baby's lips moved almost imperceptibly. Lips so small they didn't even look like lips. More like larvae, or a chrysalis that might unfold into an insect with beautiful wings. Vanishingly tiny red blood vessels coloured the skin of her cheeks beneath the peachfuzz. Kawashima stroked the surface of that fine layer of fuzz, first with a fingertip and then with the tip of the instrument.

It really is all right, I'm not going to stab the baby.

Just as he was thinking this, Yoko's soft voice shattered the silence.

'What're you doing?'

His entire body clenched, and the tip of the ice pick grazed the baby's cheek. He switched off the penlight and slowly exhaled. As he turned to face his wife, he palmed the ice pick and slipped it handle first into his pocket. She was sitting halfway up in bed, her weight on one elbow.

'Did I wake you? Sorry.'

He tiptoed to her side and leaned over to kiss her cheek.

'What time is it?' she said.

'A little past one.'

'You were looking at Rie?'

'Yeah. I didn't mean to wake you. You're tired – go back to sleep.'

'Are you still working?'

'Most of the layout is finished. I just have to choose the slides. It'll make the presentation a lot easier.'

Yoko lay back down and was asleep again before he'd even finished whispering this. Thank goodness. It would have been bad if she'd turned on the light to go to the toilet or get a drink of water. She'd have seen he was sweating, and she might have noticed the tip of the ice pick protruding from his pocket.

2

KAWASHIMA PUT THE ICE PICK away in a kitchen drawer, washed his face in the bathroom sink, and walked into the living-room. He sat at his desk and waited in vain for his heartbeat to slow down. His throat was parched with tension, and he thought about having a drink but immediately rejected the idea. He didn't allow himself alcohol at times like this, because he knew he'd just end up tossing back belts of something strong – a procedure that would help him relax only very briefly, after which he'd lose all control. He'd drink until he blacked out, and remember virtually nothing the following day.

He looked around the room, trying to breathe deeply and deliberately. They still called it the living-room but had transformed it into a work space for both of them. There were no sofas or easy chairs, but a heavy, L-shaped table of unfinished wood dominated more than half of the floor area. This monster, imported from Sweden and big enough to accommodate eight or ten dough-kneading students at once, was Yoko's most prized possession. It had been Kawashima's wedding present to her, and he'd cleaned out his bank account to pay for it.

He still felt the same about Yoko as he had back then: he couldn't believe he'd managed to meet, fall in love with, and actually marry a woman like this.

He and she were the same age. They'd met six years ago, in early summer, at an art gallery in Ginza. It was the opening of an exhibition of works by a Russian-born French artist named Nicolas de Staël, a painter of sombre abstracts. He wasn't well-known in Japan and, although it was Saturday afternoon, the two of them were the only visitors. Yoko was the first to speak.

'Are you an artist?' she said.

Kawashima was carrying a sketchbook under his arm.

'I do some drawing, yes,' he told her.

She was wearing glasses with cream-coloured frames, and they looked good on her, but he couldn't help thinking she'd be even prettier without them. They left the gallery together and went to a coffee shop with glass walls overlooking the Ginza crossing. He ordered a double espresso and she the shop's famous cheesecake and a cup of apple tea. The sun of early summer slanted gently through the blinds, and on each table was a glass bud-vase with a single orchid. Yoko smelled good. Mixed with her perfume Kawashima thought he detected another fragrance, though he didn't yet recognise it as the smell of freshly baked bread. He only knew he found it pleasant, presumably because he really liked this person and felt so relaxed around her. (Conversely, whenever he was stressed out or stuck in the company of someone he didn't care for, even ambient smells tended to strike him as repulsive.) Yoko ate her cheesecake slowly as she pored over the pages of his sketchbook. At one point a tiny crumb fell on one of the drawings, and she very carefully removed it with the corner of her napkin. Something about the way she did that made him very happy.

They began meeting about once a week to have dinner or visit a museum or see a movie together. Kawashima was working for a graphic design firm and drawing in his spare time. His drawings were all of narrow roads in the moonlight; no other subjects had ever interested him. But one day near the end of summer he drew from memory a pencil sketch of Yoko's face. When he presented the sketch to her on their next date, she invited him to her apartment for the first time. And there she made a halting and clearly painful confession. Until about a year before, she'd been dating an older man from her company, and on the day they broke up she'd swallowed a handful of sleeping pills and been rushed to the hospital. What did he think of a woman who'd do something like that? Kawashima said he didn't think it was any big deal, and he meant it.

'Who hasn't wanted to die at one time or another?' he said.

Not long afterwards, they moved in together. They'd been sharing a place for about six months when, late on a freezing winter's night, Kawashima awoke and leaped out of bed drenched in a sweat that had soaked all the way through the covers. Startled from sleep, Yoko frantically asked what was wrong, but all he would say was that he needed to take a little walk. He threw on some clothes and left the apartment. When he returned, some two hours later, he told her something he'd never told anyone before.

'I get like that sometimes,' he said. 'It's happened to me ever since I was a little kid, but I never had a name for it until I got older and found it in a psychology book. They call it *pavor nocturnus* – night terrors. It was even worse when I was little. I'd wake up in a panic and jump out of bed, like I did tonight, only I'd be screaming at the top of my lungs. Sometimes I'd run in circles around the room for, I don't know, two or three minutes. Afterwards I could never remember anything, only that something had terrified me so badly that I didn't know who I was and couldn't even recognise the people around me. It was like they'd melted into my dream, become characters in this nightmare. It was so scary. So scary. Now that I'm grown up, it's not quite as bad. I mean, I don't forget who I am anymore, and like, tonight, I knew that was you speaking to me, asking me what was wrong.'

'So why,' Yoko asked, 'did you dash out all alone? Why didn't you let me hold you?'

Kawashima shook his head.

'I've just always thought it best, when I lose control like that, not to be around anybody else. Better to go somewhere by myself and walk it off, do some deep breathing to calm myself down.'

He decided, then and there, to tell Yoko everything he'd been keeping secret for so long – with the single exception of the time, at nineteen, that he'd stabbed a certain woman with an ice pick. He didn't want to get into that, partly because the event was so vague and uncertain in his memory, and partly because he feared it might scare her away. He didn't want to lose her.

'I think what's behind them, behind the night terrors, is that after my father died, when I was four, my mother started hitting me. She'd beat the hell out of me. I don't remember my father at all, except for this vague sense that he used to take us out for drives in a car. And I know he had one, for a while at least, because my mother always used to describe him as the sort of fool who'd put a down payment on a car he couldn't afford. I haven't seen my mother for years, but the last time we met, at my high-school graduation, she said she'd treated me the way she did because I reminded her of *him* – meaning my father the fool. I was afraid of the beatings, because they really hurt, but I always just assumed she must be doing it because I was such a bad kid. The weird thing is, it's something you can learn to endure, that kind of abuse. You just tell yourself it's not really you who's getting beaten. If you concentrate really hard, you can actually get to a place where it doesn't hurt any more. A lot of times she'd beat me with no warning, and that was especially scary, so I used to try to stay prepared all the time. I'd keep reminding myself: *Mother's going to hit me, Mother's going to hit me . . .*

'What bothered me most, though, was that I was the only one she hit. She never laid a finger on my little brother. As you know, we lived in this little town in the sticks, and the nearest city of any size was Odawara. In Odawara they had a department store

12

with a Playland for little kids on the roof level. The three of us went there together a few times, but when I was about five or six my mother started locking me in the house and taking only my little brother. One time I climbed out the window and ran down the road chasing after them, and she dragged me back to the house and tied me to the water pipes in the bathroom. I remember that so clearly, like it was yesterday. I fell asleep right there on the tile floor, and when I woke up it was dark outside, and all I could see was that empty, narrow little road outside the window . . .

'Not long after that, a middle-school teacher of mine got me placed in a home for abused kids, and that's when I started drawing. Right from the beginning I drew nothing but pictures of narrow roads at night.' Kawashima bowed his head. 'I've never told anyone about this before,' he said, and Yoko took his hand and squeezed it.

They were married a year and eight months after meeting in Ginza. Yoko told her parents that in accordance with the values she and her fiancé shared she didn't want a wedding ceremony, and they reluctantly agreed. But in fact it wasn't really about values. She knew Kawashima hadn't forgiven his mother and younger brother and didn't want to put him in an awkward position.

'I was in the Home for a little over two years,' he'd told her, 'and then I went to live with my grandmother, on my father's side. At my high-school graduation, I don't know why but my mother apologised to me. It was a pretty self-serving apology but, still, it was an apology. Then, at the end, she said, "You forgive me, don't you? You forgive your mother?" I nodded without even thinking, but then something in me snapped and I slapped her face, hard. It was the only time I ever hit her.'

Kawashima hadn't opposed Yoko's decision to quit her job. He'd made up his mind right from the beginning to support her in anything she chose to do. Nor did he express any reservations when she said she wanted to have a baby. The other guys in the office often teased him about how much he'd changed since his marriage, how much more cheerful he was. 'What exactly is Yoko-chan putting in that bread of hers?' – that sort of thing. He himself wasn't really sure if he'd changed or not. But ever since he'd met Yoko, and especially since the day they'd decided, at her suggestion, to marry, his bouts of self-loathing had all but ceased. Not once had he been overwhelmed by the old panic and terror, not even when Rie was born and he first held her in his arms. Not, in fact, until ten nights ago.

The mental and emotional torment of the old cycle

of anxiety – unable to bear being alone, wanting someone always near but growing anxious when someone does get close, fearing that if they get any closer there's no telling what might happen, until the fear itself becomes unbearable and solitude seems the only solution – had seemed to be fast becoming a thing of the past.

Until ten nights ago, Kawashima muttered to himself, flicking the switch on the lightbox atop his desk. On its glass lid he arranged several of the thirty-five-millimetre slides he'd taken from the company archives. They were photos he was considering for a poster advertising the Yokohama Jazz Festival, though none of them had anything to do with jazz. Choosing graphics that had no direct connection to the product was something of a speciality of his. When the first indoor ski-slopes were about to open in Kyushu, his presentation – with copy that read THERE'S A FIRST TIME FOR EVERYTHING splashed across a photo of a little Caucasian boy and girl kissing – had won out over all the other agencies and made him a minor hero at the office. The photos he'd assembled for the jazz festival were black-and-whites of fashion models from the 1940s. The girls were all healthy specimens with generous smiles, lying on sandy beaches or about to dive into pools or strolling beneath parasols or drinking cocktails on a terrace . . .

But it was impossible to care about any of this right now.

Ten nights ago. He was in the bathtub with the baby, having just finished washing her. He handed her over to Yoko, who was waiting with a fluffy bath towel, and then he leaned back in the tub, leaving the pebbled-glass shower door partially open. Yoko was murmuring to the baby as she dried her, and he was aware of himself smiling at them. And then, with no prelude or warning, a thought came percolating up into his brain and he felt the muscles of his cheeks twitch and freeze.

I wouldn't ever stab that baby with an ice pick, would I?

For a moment, he wasn't certain who was sitting there in that steam-filled tub. Yoko opened the bathroom door to leave, then looked back and said something to him, but it wasn't registering. *Masayuki? Masayuki, what's wrong? What's the matter?* She called to him several times before he snapped out of it.

'Oh, still there? Guess I was daydreaming,' he said, and by the time his eyes were refocused on her and the baby, his skin – in spite of the very warm water – had turned to gooseflesh.

The sharp, gleaming point of an ice-pick: from that moment on, he couldn't get the image out of his head.

You wouldn't do something like that, you would never stab the baby, he told himself hundreds of times, but the voice inside him never stopped replying: *I just might*. And each night from then on he'd found himself unable to go to bed until he stood over the crib, ice pick in hand, to confirm to himself that it was all right, he wasn't going to stab her.

Kawashima turned off the lightbox. He got his leather jacket from the closet, put it on over his sweater, and headed for the door.

3

THEIR APARTMENT WAS ON the second floor of a four-storey building. He closed the door noiselessly behind him, checked several times to make sure it was locked and made his way down the stairs. There was no guard or watchman in the lobby: to enter through the glass doors you had to either punch in a code or have someone buzz you in over the intercom. To exit, of course, you simply touched the sensor plate marked OPEN, but the landlord had stressed the importance of taking precautions to prevent strangers slipping inside as you walked out. Not long before, someone apparently disguised as a delivery man had burgled one of the apartments; kids had been known to spray-paint graffiti on the lobby walls; and some jerk had once melted the intercom's plastic number pad with a lighter.

Outside, Kawashima zipped up his jacket and raised its fluff-lined collar, reflecting that he rather enjoyed the cold. In heated rooms, he often felt the outlines of his body, the border between him and the external world, grow disturbingly fuzzy.

Yoko had awakened but hadn't seemed to notice anything, and for the moment, standing on the empty street of their neighbourhood in Kokubunji, away from the room with the sleeping baby, he felt a certain degree of relief.

It's just my neurosis, he reasoned with himself. I just get freaked out *imagining* I might stab the baby. It's not as if I actually want to stab her. Who doesn't imagine things that make them anxious? Maybe nothing this extreme, but, like, having to give a speech at a wedding, for example – a lot of people are terrified of screwing up and being ridiculed or laughed at. Or you can accidentally make eye contact with some psycho on the train and think, *What if he gets off behind me and follows me home?* Thanks to the imagination, there's no end to things in this world that can trigger anxiety. Normally, of course, you can free yourself from fears like that just by facing them, or telling someone about them.

Normally.

On the ground floor of the building next door was a video shop. At the end of a long day, after dinner and a bath, Yoko liked to sit with a glass of wine or beer and watch a movie. One night in the last month of her pregnancy, the two of them had watched *Basic Instinct* together. Kawashima wanted to flee the room as soon as he saw the first scene, which depicted a murder by ice pick, but Yoko said, 'I'm not sure this is good for the baby, but it's an interesting story, isn't it?' It was that attitude of hers, that detached amusement, that helped him calm down and sit all the way through the film.

Often during the past ten days he'd wondered why his fear was of stabbing only the baby and not Yoko. Remembering the time they'd watched *Basic Instinct* together gave him the answer: because Yoko could talk to him. Talking with someone helped neutralise the power of the imagination. And Yoko had a delicate but skilful way of dealing with the wounds he carried inside. Her attitude was neither insensitive nor indulgent – neither, *Why don't you just get over it?* nor, *Oh, you poor thing!* She never went out of her way to avoid the subject, and when it came up her comments were always both clear-eyed and supportive.

'When you have a chronic illness,' she'd tell him, 'getting frustrated or impatient with it just makes things worse, right?' Isn't that what they say? That you have to live in harmony with an illness? To think of it as an old friend?'

Or: 'Why is it that when people grow up they

totally forget how vulnerable and helpless they were as children?'

Or: 'Until Rie was born, I never knew how stressful having children can be. I'm sure even your mother must wonder what she could have been thinking back then.'

The way she'd say these things never failed to soothe and comfort him. The first scene of *Basic Instinct* was a jolt to his system, but by the time the ice pick reappeared later in the film he was thoroughly enjoying the story.

In the next building past the video shop was a bookstore. Something moved in the gap between the two buildings, and he stopped to see what it was. The gap, just wide enough for a grown man to walk through, dead-ended at another building. It was very dark in there, but he was sure he'd seen two or three small figures moving. Small enough that they had to be children, no more than nine or ten years old. They weren't moving now, probably because Kawashima had stopped and was looking their way, but he wasn't about to call out to them or step over and peer into the gap. He knew that even a ten-year-old child could be dangerous. Just before walking on, he spotted a little red point of light. It might have been a burning cigarette, except for the fact that he neither saw nor smelled smoke. The eye of a small animal, maybe, reflecting the streetlight. Between the two buildings, he remembered, were garbage cans and waste water puddled around a drain. The kids were probably killing rats for kicks in that narrow darkness.

Back in the Home for at-risk children, Kawashima had had a friend his age named Taku-chan. At some point the Home acquired a pair of pet rabbits, and one of their offspring was placed in Taku-chan's care. Taku-chan loved his little pet more than anything, and even insisted on sleeping with it in his arms. But one day, right before Kawashima's eyes and for no apparent reason, he grabbed the animal by its still-undeveloped ears, stood up, and slammed it down against the concrete floor. It made a sound like delicate porcelain breaking, but the bunny wasn't dead and tried to crawl away with spastic movements, like a wind-up toy winding down. Taku-chan, wearing the same dull expression he'd often worn when stroking his pet's soft fur, stomped several times on its head with the heel of his shoe. Then, ignoring its crushed, lifeless body, he went off to get another one to take its place.

Kawashima and Taku-chan sometimes drew pictures together, and Taku-chan's were always the same. He'd smear the whole sheet of paper with black or dark blue or purple, and in the middle he'd paint a naked little boy whose body was pierced from head to foot with arrows – dozens of them protruding in every direction, like quills. 'Who's that?' a counsellor once asked him, and Taku-chan said, 'Me.' The counsellor said, 'Well, if it *wasn't* you, Taku-chan, who would it be?' 'If it's not me,' said Taku-chan, 'I don't care who it is.'

Kawashima decided he might as well head for the all-night convenience store down the street. He was walking slowly to calm himself, but his heart-beat still wasn't back to normal. The cold seeped up through the soles of his shoes, and each exhalation was a small white cloud, a visible reminder of how fast and irregular his breathing was. Across the street was an apartment building of reinforced concrete, and at the window of a corner room on the third floor a woman with short hair was smoking a cigarette. She used her sleeve to wipe a circular clear spot on the misty glass and looked down at the street. That building, Kawashima recalled, consisted entirely of studio apartments for single women. The light was behind her and he couldn't see her face, but judging by her hair-style and the way she smoked the cigarette he could tell she was no longer young. Late thirties, maybe.

The image of a hand with dry skin and wrinkles and prominent veins formed in his mind. A woman in her late thirties, holding a thin black menthol cigarette in a hand like an autumn leaf.

He'd met her when he was seventeen and lived with her for nearly two years. She was nineteen years older, and they were often mistaken for mother and son. Whenever this happened, the woman would force a smile and maintain a veneer of cool indifference; but afterwards, when she and Kawashima were alone, she'd rail bitterly against the person who'd committed the faux pas, sometimes for hours at a time. She was a stripper working in Gotanda when he met her, though in the two years they were together she must have changed clubs a dozen times.

The woman frequently brought men she'd met at her strip club back to the apartment and fooled around with them, right in front of Kawashima. If they asked, she'd tell them in a drunken mumble that he was her little brother. And yet invariably, after the men left, she'd go ballistic on Kawashima, attacking him with her fists and shrieking: 'If you really loved me! You wouldn't just sit there! And let another man! Make me do those things! You'd beat the hell out of him! Or kill him!' Eventually he did rough some of them up, after which she'd start pounding him anyway, screaming that he was going to make her lose her job. The hysteria wouldn't stop until she ran completely out of steam and passed out. What a hateful bitch, Kawashima used to think – how does a person ever get to be this despicable? He was sure he was the only one in the world who could ever care about her. Which was why he believed she would never leave him.

The night he stabbed her with an ice pick had always been somewhat unclear in his memory. He'd returned to the apartment late that night after sniffing thinner with a friend, so he wasn't exactly in a lucid state of mind to begin with. A kerosene space heater burned in the middle of the room, and a pot of water sat simmering on top of it. The woman had just got back from work and was sitting before the mirror, removing her make-up. He tried to hug her from behind, and she wouldn't let him. All she said was, 'Don't touch me,' but her manner was so cold and harsh that it terrified him. He put his arms around her again, and again she spurned him, prising his fingers loose this time and shaking him off. 'Stop breathing your fucking thinner fumes on me!' she snarled. Kawashima was devastated. All he could think was: I need to be punished. She's mad at me. She's mad at me, but she won't hit me, so I've got to punish myself. If I don't, she might leave. He walked to the heater and shoved his right hand into the pot of boiling water.

When he lifted the red, scalded hand from the pot

to show her, the woman called him a moron and walked into the bathroom, peeling off her clothing as she went. He was convinced that after her shower she'd leave the apartment. And wouldn't come back. How long would he have to sit there, scared half to death, waiting for her return? He mustn't let her go. He was racking his brain, thinking he had to do something before she finished showering, when suddenly there was a crackling of little explosions where his senses of sight and smell and hearing collided. Something like the odour of burning yarn or scorched fingernails filled his nostrils, and the next thing he knew he'd flung open the shower curtain and the tip of the ice pick in his hand was soundlessly piercing her stomach. The ice pick met no more resistance than would a safety pin sinking into a sponge. It slid effortlessly into her sagging white belly, and when he pulled it out he saw thick, dark-red blood ooze from the round little hole it had made.

The ice pick may have dropped from his scalded hand then, but his memory was pretty much a blank from this point on. He couldn't even remember if the police had shown up or not. Hundreds of times, in dreams, he'd seen the ice pick hit the tile of the bathroom floor and roll under the tub. In the dreams he'd get down on his elbows and knees and reach for it, only to burn his hand again on the pilot light for the water heater. Sometimes he'd wake up from this nightmare convinced that his right hand really was on fire. If the cops *had* come, the woman must not have told them the truth, because Kawashima was never taken in for questioning. Nor did she ever mention the incident to him, even after coming home from the hospital. He moved out without being asked. Although he returned to the apartment a number of times in the weeks that followed, the woman always refused to see him, and eventually she moved away. Kawashima believed the ice pick was probably still in that apartment, lying underneath the tub. And he somehow felt that the day would come when he'd go back there to see.

He'd reached the door to the convenience store when he noticed something curious. His heart rate had returned to normal. Wondering if this was somehow related to his reminiscences about the stripper, he stepped inside the store, where he was enveloped by the warm air and felt the outlines of his body begin to blur. He walked to the stack of shopping baskets and had just grabbed one when the clerk behind the counter to his right, silent till now, shouted, '*Irasshaimase!*' to the customers entering behind him – a young couple huddling together and gasping from the cold. The couple drifted off towards the magazine racks, and the clerk turned his gaze from them back to the register. That was all, but it was enough to trigger in Kawashima the familiar but dreadful sensation that he himself wasn't really here. Not as if he were dead or a ghost or spirit or something, but as if he'd separated from his own body and was waiting a short distance away.

As a boy, he'd escaped the pain and terror of his mother's beatings by concentrating on the thought that the one who was being hit wasn't really him. He'd consistently, methodically trained himself to think that way. His mother, enraged at the child who wouldn't cry or even cry out, only hit him all the harder; but the more she hit him, the more he concentrated on telling himself that it wasn't him she was hitting, until he actually succeeded in separating himself from the pain. Fearing, however, that if he pushed himself too far away he might not be able to find his way back, he made himself promise to wait nearby and return as soon as circumstances permitted.

What I'm feeling now, he told himself, is just a remnant of those times, just an echo from the past. He looked up at the packages of disposable diapers on a top shelf against the far wall and remembered Yoko saying that no matter how many diapers she bought it never seemed to be enough. He decided to buy some, and it was at that moment that he was suddenly convinced that he really had separated and was waiting for himself there among the diapers.

Damn, he muttered and tried to force a wry smile but failed as fear squeezed his heart. *What the hell's going on?*

He could actually see his other self standing before the shelves two or three paces ahead of him now, holding a package of disposable diapers. This other self pointed to the picture of a baby on the package and grinned at Kawashima, then beckoned to him.

Come here, there's something really important I need to tell you.

Kawashima moved towards the shelves as if being reeled in.

Think about it, the other said. *Why do you really think you were able to watch* Basic Instinct *so calmly? That's what you were wondering on the way here, right? You remembered Taku-chan too, didn't you? Taku-chan saying, 'If it's not me, I don't care who it is.' And then you remembered stabbing the woman – which calmed your heartbeat right down. It dispelled your anxiety about stabbing* this *one, right?* The other tapped on the picture, then nodded and pinched the vinyl to distort the baby's face into a grotesque mask. *Hurry up, come over here and join me.* Kawashima tried to say, *Please don't do this*, but his throat was so dry he couldn't speak. Just before the two of them merged, the other said, in a clear and distinct voice: *There's only one way to overcome the fear.*

Kawashima stood in a sort of stupor, like someone receiving a revelation from God. Even after he'd merged with his other self, the voice continued to reverberate inside him. *There's only one way to overcome the fear: you've got to stab someone* else *with an ice pick.*

4

'MASAYUKI,' YOKO SAID THE next morning as she bustled about preparing for her classes. 'Did you win the lottery or something? You're positively glowing.'

Between bites of a croissant, Kawashima explained that he'd slept like a dead man. This was true, and his appetite was back as well, much to his own surprise.

There was no way to be one hundred per cent sure of not getting caught – this had been his first thought on waking – but merely *wounding* some woman was out of the question. If she lived, she'd surely go to the police, and that would be it for him. He'd mulled over such problems while brushing his teeth and washing his face.

'You know,' he told Yoko as he dressed for work, 'our company has adopted the mandatory vacation system, like a lot of the bigger firms have?'

'You mean where you have to take time off whether you want to or not?'

'Exactly. At some of the big agencies it's for a whole month, or even two, but for us it's more like a week or ten days.'

It was a fact that Kawashima's firm had such a system – mandatory vacation for all employees once every three to five years. A fund had been set aside for that purpose, and a certain amount of cash was available for expenses, depending upon how you planned to spend your vacation.

'I've got an idea I want to work on,' he said, 'so I was thinking about taking mine soon.'

'When?'

'Like, beginning the day after tomorrow or so.'

'That *is* soon. But you're not supposed to just lie around the house, right?'

'No, and you're not to show up at the office either. You have to come up with some sort of goal, something you're going to do with your time. Not that it has to be anything that serious. One guy travelled to India, and another went to New York to check out the musicals. One of the girls flew down to Okinawa to get her scuba-diving licence.'

'Are you going overseas?'

'Here's what I was thinking. I'd like to stay in one of the major hotels downtown. You don't get a chance to do that when you live in the city, right? I'd like to stay in the sort of place where your average salarymen from smaller cities stay when they come to Tokyo.'

'What are you going to do in a place like that?'

'This might sound silly, but I want to get a better understanding of the true salaryman. Like, when I have a meeting in a coffee shop or bar in one of those hotels? I'm always fascinated by what the salarymen around me are talking about. You'd be surprised – a lot of times you hear some pretty poignant, heartfelt stuff. I'd like to make, you know, a serious study of that sort of thing, because beginning the year after next we're going to be in charge of all the graphics on a new campaign. It's for an imported car, a new model targeting salarymen in their thirties. And the fact is, I don't really know that much about your average salaryman.'

He needed a solid chunk of time in order to hone and execute his plan. But if he made up some story about having to stay near the office for days at a time to meet a deadline, for example, one phone call from Yoko to the office and he'd be busted. It was unlikely that anyone might connect that lie with a crime that took place somewhere across town, but he didn't need to complicate things by giving Yoko or the company any reason to think he was up to something fishy. Of course, staying a week at a hotel in the city for 'research' would normally be read as an affair, or a gambling problem. But he knew that Yoko would never doubt him. She wasn't the jealous or suspicious type in the first place, and in the six years they'd known each other, though he may have kept certain things from her, he'd never told her a lie. Not because he was adhering to some abstract moral principle, but simply because he didn't want to be dishonest with someone who meant so much to him. Besides, if she *should* suspect him of having an affair – well, so what?

Arranged neatly on the L-shaped table that dominated the room were all the implements Yoko needed to teach the day's classes.

'We'll have to get you packed, then,' she said with a natural, unforced smile. 'Just be sure to keep in touch. I mean, don't forget to call.'

I won't forget, Kawashima said, nodding. He walked into the bedroom and bent over the crib to peer at the baby. Lightly touching her downy cheek, he whispered, so Yoko wouldn't hear:

Everything's going to be all right.

5

FOUR DAYS LATER, KAWASHIMA was checking in at the Akasaka Prince Hotel. He used his JCB card and registered under his real name. It was a twin room with a view of Tokyo Tower in the distance, and he'd reserved it for a week. He'd never taken any serious vacation time before, and for that reason – and in recognition of his just having won the jazz festival account – the firm had immediately agreed to his request and even presented him with nearly nine hundred thousand yen in cash for expenses. His boss had joked, in typically poor taste, that the idea of observing salarymen was brilliant, but not to fall in love with one and end up with AIDS.

Kawashima checked in shortly after noon and gave Yoko a call first thing. He could hear the babble of middle-aged women in the background and could almost smell the freshly baked bread. Neither Yoko nor anyone at the office had seemed the least bit suspicious of his motives. Come to think of it, he reflected as he sat back on the sofa and gazed out at the heart of the city settling into dusk . . . Come to think of it, somewhere along the line I became a man who never does *anything* people consider suspicious. Maybe something fundamental had changed since the old days – since parting with the stripper. He'd gone back to school, taken up drawing again, found a job and met Yoko, and he often felt as if he wasn't even the same person he'd been as a teenager. But if he *was* someone different now, which of the two was the real him? *They're both the real you*, some part of him whispered, but the rest of him wasn't so sure. Sometimes the old and new selves seemed completely unrelated.

Inspired by a magazine article he'd read and photo-copied in the library, Kawashima had decided to buy a knife as well as an ice pick. The article was about a thirty-two-year-old 'soap tart' who'd been found murdered in a hotel room, with her Achilles tendons severed. An anonymous police detective had volunteered this explanation: 'When you cut the Achilles tendon, the sound it makes is as loud and sharp as a gunshot. The killer must have known that and taken pleasure in it.' Kawashima decided that before stabbing the victim's stomach with an ice pick – or afterwards, if need be – he'd slice her Achilles tendons. He was curious what it would sound like exactly. And he wanted to see the expression on the woman's face when it happened.

Thinking about these things didn't set his pulse racing or leave him staring into space, grinning and drooling. He experienced, rather, a sort of creative calm similar to his state of mind when pondering which photo to use for a poster. His heartbeat had been a problem during the ten days he'd lived in fear of stabbing the baby, but not since that night in the convenience store. Between the man who was coolly deciding to cut his victim's Achilles tendons and wondering what it would sound like, and the man who'd smiled at his wife that very morning in a room saturated with the fragrance of freshly baked bread, there was clearly a gap. Exactly what the gap consisted of he couldn't have said, but he knew there was one.

He got up and closed the curtains. From his briefcase he took the magazine article, an S&M magazine, a weekly sex-industry guide, and a notebook. He sat down at the desk and began making notes in an attempt to marshal his thoughts.

First of all, the victim would have to be a prostitute – it was the only logical choice. But what *type* of prostitute should he choose? That was important, as was the question of where the killing was to take place. He'd been hauled in by the cops once years ago for sniffing thinner, but they'd never taken his fingerprints. The cops were at a big disadvantage when a murderer wasn't acquainted with the victim and had no previous record. He'd already determined that he couldn't just stab the woman – he had to be sure and kill her. Naturally it would be best if her body were never discovered, but trying to dispose of the corpse would involve unacceptable risks. She'd have to be a freelancer, with no pimp or office or syndicate to report to. Stab her in some dark, deserted alley, maybe? Luring a streetwalker into an alley under the pretence of negotiating a price would be simple enough, but in such a dimly lit place he wouldn't have a clear view of the ice pick puncturing her stomach, and he probably wouldn't have time to slash her Achilles tendons.

Walking through the Kabuki-cho district of Shinjuku two nights ago, he'd confirmed that most of the freelance streetwalkers were from overseas, particularly South-East Asia. Among the advantages of choosing such a woman was the fact that any search for her would be half-hearted at best, since she was unlikely even to be in Japan legally. But it was essential that the flesh he pierced with the ice-pick be as white as possible. And now that he thought about it, not even a fair-skinned foreigner would do.

If the victim didn't speak Japanese well, it would be difficult to set things up properly, and, besides, it was imperative that her expressions of terror and anguish be in Japanese. Why? He wondered about that for a moment but stopped when an image of his mother threatened to form in his mind. He must concentrate only on the business at hand.

No, it would be insane to do it in an alley or park or vacant lot, or anywhere outdoors. He'd have to get a separate room somewhere. The sex businesses that would send girls to a customer's hotel room were limited to soap-tart services, erotic massage operations, and S&M clubs. As soon as the ice pick made its appearance, the woman was likely to try to flee. And to scream. She'd have to be restrained, and for an extended period of time, since she wouldn't die right away – after all, he wasn't going to be stabbing her in the heart. It would be best to watch her expire slowly, from loss of blood, but of course you couldn't get that much blood-flow from ice-pick wounds. You could cause death by internal bleeding, puncturing certain organs, but what good was that if you couldn't watch it happening?

In any case, the first step would be to get the woman tied up and gagged. That meant S&M. Apparently most S&M clubs wouldn't send their girls to 'love hotels'. The advantage of a love hotel was the shutter at the front desk that prevents the attendant from seeing your face. But the staff at places like that were always on the lookout for trouble, understandably enough, and Kawashima had read somewhere that occasionally, if a call girl's office grew concerned about a situation and phoned the hotel, someone would actually go up to the room to check on her. Besides, if anything did go wrong, the narrow little entrance and reception area would only make escape more difficult. And love hotels tended to be on quieter streets, with only scattered couples strolling discreetly up and down, so it wasn't as if you could run out and melt seamlessly into the crowd.

At a regular hotel, on the other hand, they'd see his face at the front desk, and he'd have to leave his handwriting on a registration card. But he could reserve a room using a fake name and telephone number and they'd never know the difference, as long as he checked in on time. He'd confirmed this today, here at the Akasaka Prince. He'd given them his work number and a check-in time of two o'clock in the afternoon when making the reservation, and though he waited at the office until one-forty-five, no one called from the hotel. Nor had they asked for ID. His normal handwriting was so generic that it shouldn't be a problem – provided he didn't make some idiotic mistake like leaving behind his driver's licence or business card or address book, or an envelope or sheet of paper with his company's letterhead.

A small but important detail: should he let the bell-boy help with whatever luggage he might have? The bellboy would offer to carry any type of bag, even a briefcase. Today he'd observed that Japanese guests seemed to enjoy having the boy take their bags, while most of the foreigners, perhaps because they're accustomed to having to tip everyone, tended to decline help if they could manage the luggage themselves. Well, the bellboy question was one he could resolve later. Kawashima wrote *Bellboy issue pending* and turned to a new page. He'd already filled several with crabbed, dense writing.

What sort of luggage should he carry, though? One smallish travel bag ought to do. He could leave the Prince carrying a paper shopping bag stuffed with everything he'd need and buy a travel bag on the way to the second hotel, where the actual ritual would be performed. He'd stop at one of the major train stations, or Haneda Airport for that matter, and purchase the most ubiquitous sort of bag possible at one of the little shops or stands. Preferably something cheap and mass-produced, but even a popular designer bag – a Louis Vuitton, say – would work well enough.

All things considered, one of the larger hotels

would probably be best. And when it came to interacting with the front desk, a simple disguise might be in order. But the operative word was 'simple' – it mustn't be anything that served to make him stand out in any way. Sunglasses, for example, might be effective, but he'd noticed here at the Prince that people who wore shades while checking in only drew attention to themselves. You got the impression they were trying to conceal their identities. Once the woman's body was discovered, the police would probably have nothing more than a rough composite sketch of the killer to go by. That shouldn't be too much of a threat, unless while at the hotel he were to bump into or be seen by someone who knew him. How best to minimise any danger of that happening? First of all, one ironclad rule: if while checking in he were to meet up with or even catch sight of a colleague from work, say, or one of Yoko's students – anyone whom it would be impossible to fool with a simple disguise – then the whole operation was off.

But what, specifically, would the simple disguise consist of? Parting his hair differently and wearing eyeglasses with thick lenses ought to be sufficient for the neck up. But he also had to think about clothing. After meeting someone a few times you can often recognise them even from behind, just by their body language and style of clothes. Best to buy a navy-blue or grey salaryman-style suit, of the type he never wore. And maybe a cheap overcoat. He'd have to hurry on the suit – it would take some time just to have the trousers hemmed. Shoes with insoles might be a good idea, too, to add a few centimetres to his height.

Of course, we'll need a change of clothes as well, he wrote, *since there's bound to be a good deal of blood. Taking off all our own clothes is a possibility, but it would be risky in the event of some form of active resistance on the woman's part. Besides, getting naked as the ritual was reaching a climax might be interpreted as having some sort of sexual meaning. We don't want the woman to think we're slicing through her Achilles' tendons just to satisfy a perverted sexual need. She must remain uncertain as to what significance her own bloodshed and agony hold. It's vital that those on the receiving end of violence ponder its meaning. A sad and bitter but important truth.*

Kawashima was writing thoughts down as they occurred to him, but now he stopped himself. He went back and erased everything after 'need a change of clothes as well'. In large, bold characters he wrote: *THOUGHTS IRRELEVANT TO PLANNING AND PREPARATION HAVE NO PLACE IN THIS NOTEBOOK!!*

The sun had long since set, and he looked at his

watch: eight o'clock already. It's been hours, he thought, and it feels like minutes. Had he ever been this engrossed in anything before? He took a Cola from the minibar, popped it open, and had a sip. He was beginning to feel as if any number of things he'd done and experienced in the past had helped prepare him for this mission. And to wonder, in fact, if this wasn't the end to which all the events of his life had been leading him.

He was already beginning to forget, in other words, the original motive behind the plan – to relieve his fear of stabbing the baby.

Plain jeans and a sweatshirt for the change of clothes. Nothing too baggy or bulky, however. Choose a sweatshirt of thin material. Same with the jeans. Two pairs of well-fitting leather gloves. Great care must be taken in use of gloves. Most natural to remove right-hand glove when checking in.

Fortunately no scars remained from when he'd burned his hand ten years before. No need to be too concerned about fingerprints when he checked in, either. It was unlikely anyone would remember which counter or which pen he'd used, and they'd all be covered with prints anyway. Leaving the glove on – especially while writing something – would, like sunglasses, only invite attention. It had been Kawashima's experience that whenever you were trying to hide something, others would somehow pick up on that, and surely any desk clerk would take notice of someone wearing gloves when filling out the registration card. Hotel workers were trained to be observant and adept at pretending not to be.

Assuming he declined the bellboy's help, he should take the key with his gloved hand and wear both gloves when opening the door and at all times after entering the room. He mustn't leave any fingerprints at the scene, if only to make it seem like the work of a man with a lot of experience. The police would be inclined to search for someone who had a record, and make lists of known deviants and sex offenders.

But of course he couldn't wear gloves from the time the woman arrived until he had her immobilised, for fear of arousing her suspicions. After tying her up, he'd put them back on. Poker-faced, naturally, slowly adjusting the black leather fingers, one at a time. Then the ball gag. Not one that would completely seal her mouth; she must be allowed to vocalise in a limited way. The bloodied gloves and the jeans and sweatshirt he'd stuff in separate vinyl bags, remembering first to put on the spare pair of gloves. He'd best double- or triple-bag everything, which meant he'd need to collect a number of bags from convenience stores. Cloth duct tape. Cardboard and thick paper with which to wrap the tip of the ice pick and the blade of the knife. And he'd need something to weigh the bags down when he threw them in the river – divers' weights would be ideal. Add them to the packages with the ice pick and knife as well. Once everything had been disposed of, it might be safest to leave his travel bag near a group of homeless men in a park somewhere. In which case, of course, a Louis Vuitton was out of the question.

The knife and the ice pick he'd buy at separate supermarkets in the suburbs. Preferably on Saturday afternoon or Sunday, when they were at their busiest. Did he need to do a dry run – order up a woman from a different S&M club one time before the big night, to acquaint himself with the procedure? The experience might prove useful, but there was also a slight possibility of danger. What if the first woman and the one to be sacrificed happened to be friends, for example? A long shot, maybe, but why risk it? After all, if any sort of trouble were to occur as a result of his not being familiar with S&M play, he could simply abort.

He had skipped dinner but didn't feel the least bit hungry, and was wondering why when the telephone rang. It was room service, checking to make sure he didn't want his bedcovers turned down in spite of the DO NOT DISTURB sign on his door. He said he was working and would take care of the bedding himself;

to which the clerk replied, in the most courteous tones, that bed service was available around the clock and he should feel free to request it at any time. Kawashima found himself thanking the man for his kindness, and meaning it. It felt as if even people in no way involved in his mission were cheering him on.

Turning back to his notebook, he wrote: *In addition to a simple disguise, a bit of misdirection might help*. For the hotel workers he'd interact with, maybe something basic like noisily chewing a stick of gum. Speaking with a Kansai accent, coughing frequently, limping slightly – but nothing that might prove counter-productive by leaving too distinct an impression. He'd better think this out carefully. The misdirection was an important point, and not to be ignored when it came to the final stages of the ritual either. He still hadn't decided upon a cause of death. The most orthodox method would be to strangle her. Strangling held little appeal for him; but if it came to that, he'd prefer to use a wire of thin stainless steel. Cutting her wrists or throat would be a problem in terms of the volume of blood splattered, but on the other hand a gory crime scene would help with the misdirection by pointing the police towards drug addicts or amphetamine users or the mentally ill. He could reinforce that by leaving a note with some sort of incoherent message. According to a magazine article he'd read concerning an actual incident, you could count on such communications employing words like God, Divine Will, radio waves, control, orders, commands, Heaven. He'd combine some of these into a short note. *I must do as They command*, or, *as the radio transmissions command. Behold His Divine Will*, or, *God spoke to me*, or, *I dare not disobey my orders*, or, *I have opened wide the portals of Heaven*. One of these, or some combination, would do. He could use the stationery and pen provided by the hotel. Again, no particular need to write with his left hand or otherwise disguise his writing. Just wad the note up and leave it lying in a corner of the room.

It might be a good idea to collect racing forms left behind on the train – horse-racing, bike-racing, boat-racing – and plant them in the room. Especially if he could find some from Osaka or Kobe, or a flyer advertising a loan shark or something there, and used a Kansai accent when registering. He had no time to actually make a trip to the Kansai district, but when he bought his bag at Tokyo Station or Haneda Airport he could keep an eye out for such artefacts discarded by travellers. When it came to misdirection, however, it was important to pay attention to even the smallest details. Were it to become clear that deception had been involved, the police would immediately start looking for someone rational and cunning rather than mad or desperate.

He'd choose one of the hotels in West Shinjuku, where it wasn't unusual for guests to arrive on foot rather than by taxi. The Park Hyatt, the Century Hyatt, the Washington, the Hilton, the Keio Plaza – he'd make a reservation at each of them under a different name. Then, as soon as possible, he'd go check them all out. The one with the busiest front desk and the worst service would suit him best. *Poor service*, he wrote, *means less attention focused on guests*.

He laid down the pencil and looked at his watch. It was past eleven. Yoko would be going to bed soon. He thought about calling her again but decided that twice in one day might seem unnatural. He still wasn't hungry. The little refrigerator was stocked with whisky and beer, and he felt so satisfied with the work he'd done that he decided to allow himself a drink. He took a mini-bottle of cheap domestic whisky from the refrigerator, poured it into a glass and had a sip. It was the most delicious thing he'd ever tasted.

He read over his seven pages of notes, making a few small additions, then put the notebook in his briefcase and spun the dials on the combination lock. He opened the curtains and looked at Tokyo Tower, whose lights were off now, and as he took another sip of whisky he was aware of the heat in his throat and stomach radiating waves of sexual desire through his body. After the second glass he decided not to drink any more, fearing that he might give in to the temptation to call an S&M club and have a woman sent over.

He hadn't yet decided how old the victim should be. The idea of someone in her late thirties appealed to him, but he somehow felt it would be more satisfying to plunge the ice pick into a firm, smooth young belly this time, rather than one that was soft and sagging. A young woman, yes, with resilient, snow-white skin.

As soon as Kawashima made up his mind on this point, he began to ache with desire for an older woman. The whisky-fuelled revelation that the victim should be young, after the excitement of writing out all those notes, had left him helpless with lust. Rationalising that unless he did something about it he'd never get any sleep, which would only hinder his ability to begin preparations tomorrow, he leafed through the sex guide and dialled a place that advertised *Erotic Massage by Mature Ladies*.

'Good evening. Essence Clinic.'

It was a man's voice.

'I'm at a hotel in the city. Is it too late to ask for a massage?'

He'd never called a place like this before and was surprised at how calm he managed to sound.

'Which hotel, sir?'

'The Akasaka Prince.'

'Thank you. If I may ask your room number, we'll ring you right back to confirm.'

About ten seconds after he hung up, the phone rang.

'Sorry to keep you waiting.' The man had an odd way of intoning his words. 'We have a thirty-eight-year-old widow who is available immediately.'

The voice was tranquil and mechanical and gave no sense of the person producing it. It was impossible even to imagine what the man's face looked like. Kawashima didn't answer right away, and the voice continued.

'If you wouldn't mind waiting another hour or so, however, we can send a lady in her early forties.'

'No. Send the one who can come right now, please.'

'The basic massage is 7,000 yen, and the erotic version is 17,000. Which would you prefer?'

It sounded as if the man were holding a baby as he talked. Or sitting at someone's deathbed – Kawashima pictured a shrivelled, comatose old man hooked up to an IV drip.

'Erotic.'

'She'll be at your room in approximately half an

hour. Of course we ask you to supply her with taxi fare both ways.'

Before hanging up, Kawashima ventured to ask if they got many young men requesting these older women. 'Quite a few,' the smooth voice said, and replaced the receiver so quietly that he scarcely heard the click.

What if it turned out to be *her*? It had been just ten years now, so she'd be forty-eight. The voice had said the woman was a decade younger than that, but it's not unusual for women in the sex trade to lie about their age. In fact, at the strip clubs where she was working back then, she'd told people she was twenty-eight. How many men could really distinguish ten years one way or the other, after all? If it did turn out to be her, though, what should he say? Would there still be a small round scar, or would it have healed completely by now? They'd spoken very little after she was released from the hospital, but he clearly remembered her mentioning how complicated and time-consuming the treatment was for an ice-pick wound. 'An unbelievable pain in the ass,' to use her exact words. Well, he wasn't holding any grudges. If it turned out to be her, all he needed to say was *Long time no see*. And maybe ask about the scar.

He decided to allow himself a little more whisky. After all, his urge to call an S&M club had vanished now that the thirty-eight-year-old was on her way. He opened the third minature bottle and poured it into his glass, his mind replaying the smooth voice's last words: *Quite a few*. Beyond the window-pane, veiled with condensation, was the glittering expanse of late-night Tokyo. From up here, the people on the street looked like moving dots. He'd recently watched a daytime talk show with the theme: *Young men who can love only women their mothers' age*. A psychologist in a bow-tie had expounded that 'it's a perversion of sorts, certainly, an elaboration of the so-called Peter Pan syndrome, and though the symptoms are distinct the pathology is basically the same as that of young men who sexually molest little girls; neither type has the ability to make or maintain normal, healthy relationships.' In other words, men who were attracted to much older women were sick and abnormal. If I accomplish my mission, Kawashima thought to himself, I'll go after that psychologist next, for talking such absolute shit.

The boys in the Home had rarely spoken to one another. He'd roomed with Taku-chan for two years, but it was only shortly before he was released from the place that they'd had conversations of any length. And not even then had they discussed anything very personal.

Kawashima tried to picture the boys in the Home,

to see them with his twenty-nine-year-old eyes. The playroom, its sandbox filled with white sand, all the different dolls and stuffed animals and puppets, the model tanks and cars and toy telephones, the building blocks, the little trampoline, the painting supplies, the children. He managed to envision the entire scene quite vividly: it was as if his adult self were actually standing there, watching the kids. Every imaginable trait that would make an adult despise a child could be found in someone in that room. A hundred out of a hundred grown-ups, being in close quarters with one of these children, would end up with a single thought: *What an insufferable little monster!*

These kids wouldn't say hello or answer when you spoke to them. Call to a boy repeatedly and he'd turn and stare you down, saying something like, 'Shut up, asshole, I heard you the first time.' Reprimand another and he'd go feral, throwing things and breaking toys and trying to bite your hand. Many of them ate like animals, even snatching food away from others. There were some who'd curl up in a corner, staring blankly into space only to explode into tears if anyone came near, and others as obsequious as slaves or dogs, anxiously peering up into the attendants' faces and awaiting orders. There were little girls who would snuggle up to any grown man and try to guide his hand inside their underwear, and there were kids who compulsively bit their own arms. Kids who would suddenly start twitching and banging their heads against a wall, not even stopping when the blood ran down their faces. Kids who waddled around oblivious to the stinking load in their own pants. Watching children like this, it was all too easy to see why their parents beat them. It was only natural to hate such kids, to ignore them and shower only your *other* children with love. Who wouldn't?

But of course that wasn't the way it really worked. Such behaviours weren't the *reasons* parents abused children but the *results* of abuse. *Children are powerless*, Kawashima muttered to himself. The tears rolling down his cheeks took him by surprise, and he finished the glass of whisky in one gulp. No matter how viciously they're beaten, children were powerless to do anything about it. Even if Mother hit them with a shoehorn or the hose of a vacuum cleaner or the handle of a kitchen knife, or strangled them or poured boiling water on them, they couldn't escape her; they couldn't even truly despise her. Children would struggle desperately to feel love for their parents. Rather than hate a parent, in fact, they'd choose to hate themselves. Love and violence became so intertwined for them that when they grew up and got into relationships, only hysteria could set their hearts at ease. Kindness, gentleness – anything along those lines just caused tension, since there was no telling when it would turn to overt hostility. Better to cut right to the chase by constantly eliciting disgust and anger. The asshole with the bow-tie had referred to victims of that sort of upbringing as perverts and wrote them off as pathological.

Focusing alternately on his own reflection in the bedewed window and the nightscape of Tokyo at his feet, Kawashima began to think of himself as a representative. A representative of all the children who'd become insignificant dots in that dark diorama; a martyr armed with only an ice pick, facing down the enemy hordes. Flushed with a sense of omnipotence, he summoned up the faces of the children in the Home one by one and told them: *Just wait and see*. His lips grazed the window-pane, and several drops of water ran down the glass like little bugs scattering. *I'll kill them all for you*, Kawashima muttered again and again.

6

'YOU REMIND ME OF somebody,' the masseuse said. 'I can't remember the name, but some actor. Do you know who I mean?'

She was a big-boned woman who talked a lot. She looked so little like the woman he'd stabbed ten years ago that Kawashima couldn't suppress a wry smile when he first saw her. She wore slacks of a thin, glittery material, a gaudy sweater, and a silver fox half-coat. Kawashima had, as a matter of fact, been told that he looked like certain actors or singers before. But he was sure his resemblance to any celebrity was too tenuous to be fatal, especially if he changed his hairstyle and wore glasses. He offered the woman something to drink. She asked for a glass of beer, and he got one for her and another for himself. Sipping at his beer, Kawashima asked her if it wasn't dangerous, going to the hotel rooms of men she'd never met.

'Usually you can tell if a guy's OK just by looking

in his eyes, so I haven't had any real problems personally, but some of the girls have had bad experiences. I don't mean anything *really* scary, but, like, letting guys stick their dirty fingers in there to make a little extra money and ending up with an infection or whatever. That's the sort of thing you hear about, anyway.'

Kawashima stripped, dimmed the lights, and lay face-down on top of the bedspread. The woman sat on the side of the bed and lightly ran her fingernails over his back and buttocks and hamstrings, tracing leisurely circles on the surface of his skin. He felt like a patient being pampered by a nurse. As she helped ease him over on to his back, the woman was telling him about the man she lived with, explaining that he was the one who'd bought her the fur half-coat. She placed a box of tissues next to her on the bed and rubbed oil into her left palm, then began stroking his already erect penis. He lifted his head from the pillow and asked if she wasn't going to undress as well. Without pausing the motion of her hand, she told him it would cost an extra ten thousand. 'I'll pay it,' he said, and she wiped her hand with a tissue, reminded him that he mustn't touch her, and wriggled out of her clothing.

Wanting to get a better look at her soft belly and the marks left by the elastic of her pantyhose, he switched on the bedside lamp. The woman made no attempt to conceal her body. It was a body that stirred nostalgic feelings in him: skin your fingers could sink into; breasts with visible veins and dark, downcast nipples; arms and waist and thighs that jiggled with the slightest movement; the pathos of pubic hair; the cracked, yellowed nail of a big toe. He'd once been so accustomed to this sort of body that when he first slept with Yoko the firmness of her flesh actually felt strange to him. Yoko was now twenty-nine and had given birth to a child, but when you touched her neck or arm or ass, the flesh still pressed back. Looking at the supposedly thirty-eight-year-old ass flattened against the bedspread, Kawashima thought: There's something non-threatening about skin like this. Soft as a spongecake left over from Christmas; skin that yielded to your touch rather than resisting defiantly. It was as if the very cells were conscious of their age and had ceased to assert themselves.

He was drinking this body in with his eyes when he came. The woman wiped him off with a hot, wet towel.

After handing her over 30,000 yen and sending her on her way, he lay back on the bedspread, still naked. He was enveloped in a sort of weightless tranquillity that was like nothing he'd ever experienced before. Far from any danger of his nervous system going haywire. Kawashima had never understood the how or why of those episodes of his – the explosions of shock and terror and rage, the total loss of control – but they always left him feeling miserable afterwards. He'd often wondered if one couldn't train oneself to develop nerves that wouldn't crack like that. But the reality, he thought, staring up at the ceiling, is that I'll probably have to go through this sort of thing forever. He'd just spurted a large volume of semen, and though it had occasioned him no more excitement than a good sneeze, he was enjoying the after-effects. It felt good just lying there gazing at the ceiling. He was aware that the good feeling existed side by side with a chilling sort of loneliness, but even that wasn't all bad. He was picturing the masseuse's bulky thighs when something important occurred to him, and he sat up in bed and reached for his briefcase. He opened it, took out the notes, and added a couple of lines:

The woman must be not only young but petite. A large woman would be more difficult to control in the event of any unforeseen glitches.

7

SANADA CHIAKI WAS AWAKE but needed to lie in bed a while longer. The dial on her electric blanket was turned to high, but because of the Halcion she felt heavy and frozen stiff, from hair to toenails. The phone stopped ringing, and after the high-pitched mechanical whine of her answering machine a subdued male voice eased out of the little speaker.

'Aya-san, are you going to make it to the office today? Either way, give us a call, will you? If you're not feeling well, you can have the night off, of course, but we need you to call in. We've got you down for an appointment this evening, six o'clock at the Keio Plaza, room 2902, a Mr Yokoyama. He's a new client, but he sounds young, and he sounds like a gentleman. You'll probably have to go straight there, considering the time, but drop by the office when you finish, no matter how late it is, all right? And please don't turn off your—'

A beep signalled an end to the allotted message time. A few moments later the phone rang again.

'I got cut off. As I was saying, we need you to leave your pager on. If you pick up this message from outside and don't have your toys with you, you'll have to stop by the office or your apartment first. Whatever you do, don't show up at the appointment without equipment, all right? Anyway, we're waiting to hear from you. If you're running short on time, you can call after you've arrived at the Keio Plaza. Your period hasn't started yet, has it? If it—'

The machine cut him off again, and this time he didn't call back. Chiaki decided she'd better get up and eat something. She looked at the clock and saw that it was already three in the afternoon. The Keio Plaza was only twelve or thirteen minutes away by taxi, but after a three-Halcion sleep she'd need time just to get her blood circulating again. She'd been gradually increasing the dosage recently and knew she'd have to watch that. The pills weren't cheap, and someone had said that the shop in Shibuya where she bought them was under investigation.

She rolled on to her side and reached for the CD player remote. She hit POWER, saw the little green light come on, and pressed PLAY. It wasn't the CD she was expecting. She liked to listen to strings first thing on awaking and could have sworn she'd put in a Mozart disc before going to sleep, but oozing out of the speakers now was the theme song from *Wild at Heart*, with a tenor sax that dripped like molasses over her nerve endings. It was music she liked to listen to when masturbating. It's weird I don't remember, she thought as she turned off the music – and what if it's not just because of the sleeping pills? The thought triggered a wave of anxiety, and she decided to try to recall exactly what she'd done before going to sleep. According to the clock it was Friday, which meant she'd been asleep for about fifty hours straight. She'd taken the Halcion late Wednesday morning, after an all-night job for which she'd received 150,000 yen. She hadn't taken the money to the office yet, either, which explained why the manager was so insistent about her calling in.

The client had been a mild, middle-aged man who after half-heartedly tying her up and poking her with the vibrator had taken her hand and asked her to sleep next to him. She wasn't sleepy, and because she was concerned about her libido having gone missing the past month or so, and because he wasn't a type she found repulsive, she'd been prepared to have normal sex with him, as long as he used a condom. So naturally this was the one time the client just wanted to sleep by her side. He fell asleep right away, with his mouth open, and she couldn't bear even to look at him. He wasn't a smoker, but his breath was bad and smelled faintly of alcohol, and soon he was snoring loudly without loosening the tight grip he had on her hand. He hadn't paid her yet, so she couldn't have left anyway, but her muscles tensed up when she tried to lie still, and the more she told herself she had to sleep, the more it felt as if someone had turned a spotlight on her brain.

Don't tell me it's starting up again, she remembered thinking, and the thought had terrified her and made her think it really was starting up. Any minute now she'd become aware of What's-her-name lurking up there at the corner of the ceiling, staring down at the man and her.

What's-her-name had first appeared when Chiaki was in middle school. In the beginning, she'd begged her not to look, but What's-her-name would just snicker, in a voice that apparently only Chiaki could hear.

This time, as it turned out, What's-her-name never did materialise, but because her handbag was out of reach Chiaki couldn't get to the Halcion and had to lie there until dawn, wide awake. By then her muscles were so rigid it hurt, and she was scared. But what really tormented her was the fact that she couldn't detect so much as zero point one milligram of sexual desire anywhere in her body. If this had happened in the old days, before she'd changed her personality, she probably would have shaken the man awake and demanded sex.

She wasn't like that any more, though. She'd revamped her personality on the hundred and twenty-fourth day after her eighteenth birthday, the year she graduated high school and entered junior college. In junior college she'd had just one friend with whom she'd go out for tea and share lecture notes and so on, and when she told her about it this girl had said, 'No way! Is it even *possible* to change your personality overnight?'

I did, Chiaki told herself. I changed my personality just like that. I became modest and reserved, even a little withdrawn, and after that there were lots of people who wanted to be my friend. Not that we necessarily stayed friends very long, but still, I made the change because I realised something: that the sex you have with a man at your own suggestion is just never that good. After all, if you have to ask for sex, it means the man isn't really into it, right? And guys are never sweet or gentle or thoughtful in bed if they're not really into it. There's nothing cute about their faces when they come, either, and you end up wondering what's the point of rubbing your flesh and organs together like that, having this thing flopping around inside you. It makes you feel even lonelier than if you were alone. And then, after he comes, the man makes an even worse face. *What am I doing with a slut like this?* That's what the expression on his face says.

A slut like this, Chiaki muttered, imitating a gruff, masculine voice as she struggled up on to her elbows. *How low can you get?*

Looking down at her T-shirt, she could see the outline of the nipple ring. She'd done the piercing herself seventy-one days ago. It had hurt when she pushed the needle through, and again when she pulled it out, but it had been a total success. After about a week all the pain was gone. And by the thirty-third day not a trace of scabbing or scarring remained. Chiaki was proud of herself. And the guys at the body-art shop in Shibuya, a hundred and sixty-three steps from the entrance to Tokyu Hands, had been so helpful and nice. Next she wanted to get a tattoo. To be able to choose your own pain – it's a little scary, she thought, but it's wonderful, too. She tugged at the neck of her T-shirt and peeked down at the ring.

Her clients lately had all been of the worst sort – men who weren't interested in the more exciting types of play but only in getting their rocks off as quickly as possible. In private life she'd been dating three different guys, but each of them had stopped calling recently, for various reasons – like the way she tended maybe to overreact when they messed up her room. Judging from the *Wild at Heart* CD and the fact that she wasn't wearing panties, she must have masturbated before sleeping, probably for a long time. She seemed to recall it vaguely: spurred on by her desire to feel desire when there was nothing there, reaching for it until her own moaning sounded fake to her and she began to fear that it would turn into someone else's voice altogether, but being spared that when the third Halcion tablet kicked in and sucked her down in a whirlpool of sleep.

Things had not been going well lately. She stroked the silvery ring with her index finger and thought: This is all I can really believe in right now. Even when she caressed it herself, it felt like someone else's touch. It was a fourteen-gauge surgical stainless steel ball-closure ring with an inner diameter of twelve point seven millimetres. 'What're you, nuts?' her customers often asked her. 'Why would you do that to yourself?' Piercings scared them, like tattoos on yakuza thugs, and inwardly Chiaki would sneer at these men: *Because I enjoy watching worms like you squirm.*

She was thinking she'd have to pierce the other nipple sometime soon, when the blood finally began coursing through her Halcion-frozen body. A piercing took courage, though. First she'd need to reclaim her sex drive. Not that being horny made you brave, but the total absence of lust frightened her because it had always been the first stage of that awful cycle, the one she'd never been able to tell anyone about. The cycle of terror that took hold with the sudden realisation that she alone was to blame for all the bad things happening around her. Once the Nightmare began, she wouldn't be choosing her own pain any longer – it would be choosing *her* – and courage would be the last thing she'd be capable of.

She climbed out of bed and stood there on the carpet for a moment, checking herself for dizziness or nausea. She found both, naturally, along with a chill that vibrated in her bones. What she needed was some vitamin C and stomach medicine. She took a step towards the refrigerator, measuring her stride so that she'd arrive in precisely five steps. She could pour some Vittel mineral water into the 8,935-yen Baccarat tumbler she'd bought a hundred and eighteen days ago, then drop in some cherry aspirin and two Alka-Seltzers. Just watching the millions of tiny bubbles might calm her down some, she was thinking, when she reached the refrigerator and noticed her shiny red Swiss Army knife in a wicker bowl on the dining table. Knife, scissors, can opener, bottle opener, corkscrew, file – it had everything. I have to remember to take that with me, she thought. She'd been forgetting about what the customer she'd had a hundred and seventy-one days ago had shown her. With surgical precision, he'd used a pair of scissors to extract the elastic band from a plastic shower cap. He positioned the elastic band between her legs and passed a rope through the loops, front and back, then tied the rope around her waist, making a sort of open-crotch thong. He arranged it so that only her clitoris was protruding between the strands of elastic. That was exciting. Maybe if she did it again, her libido would have no choice but to come rushing back. Before opening the refrigerator, Chiaki slipped the knife into her handbag.

8

KAWASHIMA LOOKED AT HIS wristwatch for about
the twentieth time, checking it against the digital clock
embedded in the side-table, but it was still only two
minutes past six. No reason to expect a woman in
that line of business to be punctual, of course. She
was coming by taxi, and an unexpected traffic jam
could easily eat up half an hour. Even the masseuse
he'd called the other night had been almost forty
minutes late, after all. He kept telling himself things
like this, but it wasn't doing much good.

He had turned off the heat a while ago, and the
room was cooler now, but his hands were still perspir-
ing. The brand new black leather gloves looked slightly
ridiculous with sweat soaking through the palms. He
decided to review his notes, to make sure he hadn't
forgotten anything vital.

So far everything had gone like clockwork. He'd
taken a hotel bus from the west exit of Shinjuku Station

and arrived at the entrance to the Keio Plaza right on schedule, at two-fifty-five. It was Friday afternoon and an auspicious day according to the lunar calendar, which made for a lot of weddings. The lobby swarmed with reception guests, and since the hotel was also hosting a gathering of Shinjuku-ward accountants and a conference for computer manufacturers, the counters at the front desk were swamped. Kawashima scarcely drew a glance from the beleaguered and somewhat grumpy desk clerk, and none of the bellboys got anywhere near him. He scoured the crowd in the lobby but saw no one he knew.

The room, on the twenty-ninth floor, looked out on the Tocho – the soaring new Municipal Government Office complex. The ice pick and knife and change of clothes were in paper sacks inside the overnight bag he'd bought at a shop in Haneda Airport – a dark brown synthetic leather bag like you might find anywhere. He'd changed into the cheap new suit and donned the glasses inside a stall in the airport restroom, and had managed to find a discarded sports daily from the Kansai district. Because of the crush in the lobby, he'd exchanged only a few words with the clerk when checking in, and though he'd used a Kansai accent, it was unlikely the clerk would even remember that. Whether to proceed with the misdirection scheme by leaving the sports daily in the room was something he could decide later on, after it was all over.

Reviewing the notes helped calm him somewhat. He looked out at the Tocho, with its hundreds of lighted windows. On the street below was a tour bus from which family groups had spilled out to take photos and videos with the futuristic building as backdrop. From beyond the glass came a sound like a brewing storm. The winter solstice was near, and it was shockingly cold out there, but these tourists from the hinterlands didn't seem to mind. He could see their scattered camera flashes, like the last bursts of life from the firework sparklers of his childhood. Since getting together with Yoko the sensation hadn't been quite as pronounced, but even now, whenever he saw families together, a cold little wave seemed to ripple through him. This wave was now lapping against his memory banks, uncovering an image from the past. Mother smiling as she poses the beloved little one for photos in front of the house. It's a sunny day, but she's using a flash. The beloved one waving me over to pose with him. I shake my head, and now Mother's smile vanishes. Holding the camera in both hands, she turns to stare at me with empty eyes. *Get angry*, I'm thinking. *Hurry up and hit me*. She just stands there with that stony expression. *Come on*, do *it*. Staring right through me, as if I were a piece of furniture or a rock or bug rather than a human being.

To sweep this image from his mind, Kawashima tried to conjure up the firm white abdomen of the young woman who was presumably making her way to his room. On the phone, the man at the S&M club had said she was petite and fair-skinned and a bit shy. This man's voice and way of speaking had been very much like that of the man at the massage service. As if he were sitting at someone's deathbed. If a voice like that were to tell you there was nothing to worry about, Kawashima thought, you'd almost certainly begin to panic. He looked at his watch. More than twenty minutes past six. He thought of Yoko but knew he couldn't phone her, because the hotel computer would record all his calls. Best to forget about Yoko anyway, until the ritual was over. The person staying in this room wasn't Kawashima Masayuki, but Yokoyama Toru. As he repeated this made-up name beneath his breath, he almost began to believe that that was who he really was – a different person, with a different history.

He'd just begun to consider phoning the S&M club when the door chime sounded. On his way to the door, Kawashima stopped at the thermostat to turn on the heat. The room needed to be warm enough for her to be comfortable taking off all her clothes. He removed and pocketed his gloves and took out a handkerchief to palm in his right hand.

9

It seems like forever since I've been to one of the big hotels, Sanada Chiaki was thinking as she gazed up at the cluster of highrises in West Shinjuku. S&M hotels, with their floors dotted with hardened globs of candlewax, tended to take all the romance out of things. For tonight's client, whom the manager had described as a gentleman, she was wearing her Junko Shimada one-piece mini with black stockings and a beige cashmere coat, and she'd taken extra pains with her make-up. In order not to be late, she'd boarded a taxi in front of her building in Shin-Okubo at twenty to six. Traffic was a little congested on the big overpass, but she'd still arrived at the entrance to the Keio Plaza with five minutes to spare.

People were queued up outside the entrance waiting for taxis, and luckily the doorman was busy herding them into their rides and didn't approach her. It always made Chiaki nervous when some big doorman with braid on his shoulders came up and said, 'Welcome to the Such-and-such Hotel, may I take your bag?' She'd removed the batteries from the vibrator, and all her toys were in separate opaque vinyl pouches in case anyone saw inside her bag, but still. There was something about the way doormen looked at you.

The lobby was packed with people emerging from a big wedding reception. They were dressed in formal suits and gowns and kimonos and holding gift bags embossed with the name of the hotel, and their voices reverberated off the ceiling and walls so loudly that Chiaki couldn't even hear her own footsteps. She headed towards the public telephones to call her office, having decided that if the client was a first-timer, as the manager had said, he might be put off by her making that call right in front of him. 'I've arrived at the gentleman's room' – it just sounded so cold and mercenary.

All four of the green pay phones were in use. As she approached them, she got out her wallet and extracted a telephone card – the one with the cartoon bunny. She stopped a short distance from the bank of phones and was trying to guess which of the four people would finish first, when she noticed the man on the second phone from the right leering at her. He was in his late thirties or early forties, wearing an overcoat with prominent stains, and he was looking her up and down and grinning. But no sooner had she noticed him than, without warning, he began yelling into the mouthpiece, so loudly that the people on either side of him flinched and turned to look. 'Just shut up and take care of it, bitch!' he shouted and slammed the receiver down as if he meant to break it.

Chiaki stood there thunderstruck, petrified by the instantaneous transformation from leering grin to violent, red-faced rage. When the man spun on his heel and marched towards her, it was only by tensing every muscle in her body that she managed not to scream. She didn't notice that the telephone card had slipped from her fingers until the man bent down before her to pick it up. As he stooped, she turned and staggered away, her body stiff with tension.

It's no one I know, I've never met or even seen him before, there's nothing to worry about, she told herself, suppressing the urge to run. Where to go? She no longer knew which hotel this was or even why she was here. After twenty-one steps she stopped to look back. She was surrounded by people in suits and gowns and had to stand on tiptoe to scan the room for the man in the overcoat. Not seeing him anywhere, she began to breathe again and ploughed ahead in search of a restroom. She wanted to be alone, somewhere her pounding heart would have a chance to settle down.

In the restroom she entered a cubicle and sat on the closed lid of the toilet seat, still wearing her coat. She didn't understand what was happening. Again and again she reminded herself that she didn't know the man in the overcoat, had never met him. But his outburst had brought her to the verge of remembering something. It was as if all the little clumps of dormant memories stashed in various parts of her body had wriggled to life at once.

Her pulse wouldn't slow down. She stood up and shed the cashmere coat, hanging it from a hook on the stall door. She closed her eyes and tried to chase away the image of the man on the phone by touching her dress where it covered the nipple ring. The material of the Junko Shimada was too thick for her to catch the ring between her thumb and finger, but she managed to confirm the hard, metallic feel of it, a faint reminder of the pain she'd felt the night she did the piercing. *Help me*, Chiaki whimpered, stroking the outline of the ring. This was what always happened when she lost her sex drive for any length of time: something would jog those sleeping memories and set off a terrifying sequence of events. Still stroking the ring, she thought: *I want to be some-*

where else. And in the instant of thinking this, she remembered where she was.

It's the Keio Plaza Hotel, and a gentleman is waiting for me on the twenty-ninth floor.

She looked at her watch. It was almost six-twenty. Maybe, she thought, the young gentleman would help get her sex drive going again, and all the little memories would go back to sleep.

10

'I'M AYA,' THE GIRL said when Kawashima opened
the door. He noticed that she turned her head to look
down the corridor before stepping inside.

'Hello.' Using his handkerchief, he shut the door
and set the chain lock. He'd already hung the DO NOT
DISTURB sign on the outer knob. The girl apologised
for being late and asked in the same breath if she
could use the phone.

Chiaki sized up the room as she called the office
to report her arrival. It was a twin, but surprisingly
spacious. Wearing a cheap suit like that but staying
in an expensive room like this, she thought – weird.
But his face was all right; in fact he was more or less
her type, really. Not fat, and not a slob. Why was he
holding that stupid handkerchief, though?

'May I ask for something to drink?' she said after
hanging up.

Kawashima found it unsettling that the girl kept

looking back at the door. He used the handkerchief to open the minibar and remove a slim can of Cola, his mind racing with anxious thoughts. What if someone was waiting outside for her? Or if a security guard had stopped her and asked a lot of questions?

He nodded towards the door as he handed her the Cola and said: 'Is anything wrong?'

'Wrong?' Chiaki said, thinking: Why don't you mind your own business, Mister? She took a long drink, draining half of the slender can.

'You seem to be watching the door,' he said. 'Did something happen out there?'

She was certainly petite enough, and her skin could scarcely have been whiter.

'No. Just . . .' Chiaki didn't want to risk remembering the man in the overcoat, so she decided to make something up. 'I went to the restroom? Downstairs? And there were these two ladies talking to each other in sign language, and I've always thought sign language was really pretty to watch, so I was watching them, and after that we were in the elevator together, too, and they were still talking, I mean signing. It makes a big impression on you, though, don't you think, when you see people talking without their voices? So, I don't know, I guess I was thinking about them still out there, you know, chatting away without saying anything?'

She was proud of herself for coming up with this lie on the spur of the moment. It was based on a real incident, too. Eighteen days ago she really had watched two women communicating in sign language, at her local supermarket, and it really had made a big impression on her. The supermarket had been crowded and noisy, but a peaceful bubble of silence seemed to surround the two women. A beautiful lie, she thought – maybe even too good for a man in a cheap suit and shoes to match.

'Sign language, eh?' Kawashima muttered. He looked the girl over, wondering why she'd invent such a ridiculous story.

She was well-groomed, at least, with nice hair and decent taste in clothing. Petite but well-proportioned. Small face, symmetrical features. Softly spoken and courteous enough. But her eyes were restless, and a little glassy. Near-sighted, maybe? It wasn't that she avoided his gaze exactly, but that her eyes didn't seem to stay focused on anything. As if they were disconnected from her consciousness. She might have been sitting in a room by herself, talking to a chair.

She's scared, Kawashima suddenly realised. But what was she afraid of? And why did she need to lie? In any case, it would be best to get her immobilised as quickly as possible.

'I've never tried S&M before,' he said, 'so I'm not

sure what I'm supposed to do exactly, but . . . I can ask you to take off your clothes and let me tie you up, right?'

Chiaki had been relieved that his face seemed all right, but now her guard went up. For all she knew he might turn out to be the worst possible sort. What if, far from stimulating her libido, he ended up waking those memories, like the man in the overcoat? The thought frightened her. And what was with that handkerchief? He seemed manly enough otherwise – why was he holding a hanky like some old lady at a funeral?

'It helps if we sit and talk awhile first,' she said. 'To break the ice? And find out, you know, what we both like and everything?'

'Fine. What shall we talk about?'

Kawashima glanced impatiently at his watch. It was nearly seven. Considering all there would be to take care of when the ritual was over, he was eager to get things rolling as soon as possible. But he had to avoid making her uneasy or suspicious.

'Anything, really. Tell me what you like. Or, for example, what's the nastiest thing you've ever done?'

She'd have to teach the man in the cheap suit how to get her hot, and how exciting it could be for both of them if they used an elastic band down there, with just her clitoris sticking out for him to look at and lick and touch.

The nastiest thing you've ever done – Kawashima felt queasy just hearing the words, which immediately evoked a picture of the woman he'd stabbed with the ice pick. Beating the stuffing out of each other, to the point of exhaustion, then crying and begging each other's forgiveness, caressing and kissing the sores and scratches and bumps and bruises as they peeled off each other's clothes – that was the way she liked it. Sometimes, when she connected with a solid punch, he'd think: In a minute she'll be licking that very same spot. He looked at the girl's smooth, unwrinkled hands. He couldn't wait to cut her Achilles tendons.

'Have you ever watched a woman masturbate?'

Chiaki smiled as she said this, then ran her tongue over her lips. She imagined that the cheap suit had never done *anything* nasty outside of a strip club or 'soapland' or whatever. The first thing she had to do was put him in the mood. Peering steadily at his face, she shifted on the sofa, lifting the skirt of her Junko Shimada and hanging one knee over the armrest, showing him the purple panties beneath her black stockings. She touched a finger to her tongue, as if to lubricate it with saliva, then lightly stroked her inner thighs. He's probably never seen anything like this before, she thought. I'll get you so worked up, Mister, that juice will ooze out of your willy and stain your cheap underpants. After that, we'll take a shower

87

together, and I'll teach you about the elastic band on the shower cap.

Strange shoes, thought Kawashima. Short, lace-up boots that covered the ankle bone. Black, with stiletto heels. He'd have her put them back on before he tied her up. Push forward on the heels to stretch her Achilles tendons, then press the blade of the knife down hard and slowly slice through. He wondered what would happen to the shoes then. Would they just sag forward, or would the recoil of the tendons send them flying?

The girl closed her eyes and began to moan. In those black stockings, her legs looked incredibly delicate and slender. Not much meat even on her thighs and ass, he noted. When she was done, he'd ask her in a very gentle and patient tone of voice to undress. What a lame performance, though, he thought and laughed to himself. Someone must've told her that johns get off on watching things like this.

Chiaki was tracing her finger along the crease in her panties when she heard the man laugh. She opened her eyes, and he was sitting there in his cheap suit, holding the handkerchief to his mouth and chuckling.

'That's enough,' he said.

Humiliated, she immediately swung her leg down from the armrest, and as she did so her heel struck the coffee table with a bang, knocking over the can of Cola. Kawashima reflexively grabbed the can with his bare left hand.

'Idiot!' he shouted, staring bug-eyed at the can he was holding and feeling as if his temples had burst into flame. 'Watch what you're doing!'

Chiaki's heart gave a hard thump and began to flutter. A pale mist blurred her field of vision. She'd been trying to arouse him but had only succeeded in making him angry. It was all her fault, and she found herself unable to fight off the eddying panic. Like lights going out one by one, words were whirling away, receding out of reach. *AROUSE, MASTURBATE, SEX,* then *CHEAP SUIT, HUMILIATED, SIGN LANGUAGE, RESTROOM* . . . It was as if neon signs in the shapes of all these words were slipping off into darkness and memories were rising to take their place. This was the scariest part – the sudden anticipation of the Nightmare to come. Once the Nightmare began, of course, there wouldn't even be anything you could recognise as fear.

My make-up, she thought. I've got to fix my make-up.

Kawashima didn't know what was happening to the girl, but *something* was, and it was unnerving to watch. Had he made her angry by laughing at the masturbation act and then shouting at her? Her face was a blank mask, and her eyes seemed to bob freely in their sockets, focused on nothing. He was about to say something to her when she suddenly reached for the handbag at her feet, placed it on her lap, dug around inside, and extracted a tube of lipstick. She then calmly proceeded to apply it to her lips, peering into a compact she held in her left hand. So she's not angry, he thought, feeling mildly relieved. He didn't notice the tip of the lipstick trembling, or the resulting slightly uneven line.

She put the lipstick and compact back in her bag and stood up.

'I'll just take a shower,' she said.

There was something different about her voice now too.

'Will you let me tie you up after that?'

'Anything you like!' she said and giggled. Tucking the handbag under her arm she made her way to the bathroom, went inside, and shut the door behind her.

What was she doing in there? Thirty minutes had passed since the girl had painted her lips red and disappeared into the bathroom. Kawashima had carefully and repeatedly wiped the Cola can clean of any fingerprints, and all the implements necessary for the ritual were in place. He'd already put on a new pair of leather gloves and unwrapped the knife and ice pick, picturing the girl's slender legs as he did so. Her waist would be slender too, her stomach flat. He'd bought the longest ice pick he could find – the metal part was fifteen or sixteen centimetres long – and it might just pierce all the way through her. His intention had been to tie her to the sofa, but he'd better rethink that or he wouldn't be able to see the point of the ice pick protruding out of her back. To suspend her from the ceiling, with just the tips of her toes touching the floor, would be ideal, but it wouldn't be possible in this room. There was nothing to attach a rope to.

His heartbeat quickened as these thoughts raced through his mind. He was leaning against the wall in the vestibule outside the bathroom now, taking the gloves off and putting them back on and growing agitated. What the hell was she doing in there – shampooing, maybe?

What bothered him most was the faraway look he'd seen in the girl's eyes. Those restless, disconnected, oddly glazed eyes. It seemed to Kawashima that he'd met a woman with eyes like that before, but he didn't try to remember who she was. He had nothing but unpleasant memories of all the women in his past, with the single exception of Yoko.

'You all right in there?' he said, knocking on the bathroom door.

I'm fine! came the reply. *Just a little while longer!* The voice was high-pitched and the intonation oddly warped, like a cassette tape coming unreeled. He could still hear the shower.

My lipstick's crooked, Chiaki had thought when she first looked in the bathroom mirror. You have to take extra special care with lipstick. She rubbed violently at her mistake with a tissue, pressing hard enough almost to bruise her lips, but they'd already lost the capacity to feel anything. She took off her dress, folded it, shook it out and refolded it several times before setting it on the counter next to the sink, then went through the same routine with her slip. She turned on the shower and slowly twisted the handle from C to H until the air filled with steam, then felt the water with her hand and gave a little cry. It was scalding. She turned the handle slowly back towards C before checking the temperature again, cupping the other hand under the water. She went back and forth between H and C a dozen or more times, alternating hands, and then returned to the mirror, leaving the shower running and steam billowing into the room.

As she undid her bra, she remembered that she'd been in high school when the Nightmare first happened. It was only at times like this, when it started up again, that she could really remember what it was like.

Her second year of high school. She and some classmates had gathered at the house of one whose parents weren't home, and they'd ended up watching a pornographic video. The tape hadn't been rewound and came on in the middle of a hardcore sex scene. She didn't know how long she'd watched it, but she remembered that at some point her stomach had begun to hurt and then, suddenly, she was consumed with a nameless terror. It was as if someone were flashing a strobe light in her face, and a completely different scene unfolded before her eyes.

That was the first episode, but now she'd been visited by the Nightmare a total of seven times. Losing her sex drive, it always started with that. She knew she was in trouble when she could look at a really hot guy without thinking where she'd like to lick him, or where she'd like to feel his tongue. The blood vessels or nerves or whatever would shut down, and all the hungry yearning, no longer able to make its way to the surface or connect with her libido, would begin accumulating deep inside – though she couldn't have said exactly where. And this condition would continue for the longest time. Once, it had gone on for nine hundred and thirty-eight days. To cope with the anxiety, she'd sometimes try to have sex with someone – *any*one – but it always felt as if the man's penis wasn't in her vagina or anus but a completely different sort of hole. Orgasm was out of the question, and there were even times when she ended up not knowing where she was or what she was doing. Or, worse yet, she'd have the creepy sensation that What's-her-name was up on the ceiling, watching.

Of course, Chiaki thought as she rolled her panties down, I know perfectly well who What's-her-name is. What's-her-name is me, watching myself have sex. At first I used to ask her not to look at me like that, but all she would do is snicker, so I stopped. Besides, I was afraid that if I talked to her too much I might divide into two separate people.

She thought about the man in the cheap suit, and wondered if he was a cleanliness freak. He never let go of that handkerchief, she thought, not even for a second. Men like that are sick. What they really love is dirty stuff, and doing disgusting things. You-know-who was like that, too. You-know-who? Wait a minute. Who am I thinking of? He always wore a newly laundered and starched white shirt, with trousers creased to perfection, and no matter where he went he had his white handkerchief. Somebody once teased him about that, saying he looked like an old lady at a funeral, but he said a starched white shirt and clean white hanky always made him feel that even his heart was as pure and clean as the driven snow.

He was my father. He liked to do filthy things. When I was in elementary school he even told me not to bathe. *I really love you, Chiaki. So I want to lick all the dirt off you myself. It might feel really good, but there's nothing to be afraid of. You mustn't tell anyone about this, though. It's our secret. Don't even tell Mama. If anyone finds out, they'll take you away from Mama and me, so never, ever tell anyone, OK?*

But I did, finally. In middle school I told my friend about it, and then I told Mama too. Mama talked to him, and he was standing there in his white shirt, twisting his white handkerchief and listening to all these things she was saying, and then suddenly he started yelling at me. *How dare you make up such a disgusting lie!* That was the first time I ever heard him raise his voice, but it certainly wasn't the last. After that, he turned into a different person, someone who was always yelling about every little thing. *My heart is as pure and clean as the driven snow. Pure and clean as the driven snow. Pure and clean as the driven snow.* Don't make me laugh.

'No more words,' Chiaki muttered to herself, and just then a voice spoke to her from beyond the door.

'You all right in there?'

'Fine!' she called out. 'I'm fine. Just a little while longer!'

Just a little while longer and all the words would be gone. It was only when you actually experienced words vanishing that you realised how dry and life-less they were, like dead leaves or old, discarded money. You could spend hours flattening out all the wrinkles and creases, but when you tried to buy something with those bills, no one would accept them. They wouldn't even take you seriously. You clench your fist in anger, and the bills just crackle and crumble apart in your hand.

Just before words vanish they acquire a sickening pulpy smell, like clumps of dead grass whipped by the wind into dry little spheres, and they spill from the brain and the vocal cords, down through the blood vessels and nerves to the deepest, farthest corners of your body. Words the size of pachinko balls or Tic-Tacs, vanishing as they roll off into the hidden crannies, where they bump into these other things and awaken them. These memories.

Memories aren't like words; they're soft and gooey. Covered with a sticky slime, like a penis after sex, or your vagina when you menstruate, and shaped like tadpoles or tiny watersnakes. When these sleeping memories are awakened, they begin to squirm and then to swim, slowly at first but gradually faster, up to the surface. And once they get there, your senses shut down. The first wave hits you in the lips, then the palms of the hands, the toes, and under the arms. Some of the memories escape through the pores of your skin to hang about your body like a mist, waiting for the rest to swim up and join them. Once they're all there, they come together to form an image, and it's like a television screen being switched on before your eyes.

His face as he licks me down there. His face. A face like a bundle of rotting vegetables wrapped in an old rag. *I love you,* he whispers. He keeps whispering this as he licks and licks and licks. *I love you. I love you. I love you, Love you. Love you. Love you. Love you. Love you. Love you.* Then another voice, blending with his. A little girl's voice. My voice.

Chiaki tugged on her nipple ring. She felt nothing, no pain whatsoever. She tugged harder, until her breast stood out like a little teepee and a tiny amount of blood oozed from the hole that passed horizontally through her nipple.

The sound of the shower was like the hissing static of an untuned radio. Kawashima was slipping past irritation into anxiety. He stood in front of the bathroom door and checked his watch: she'd been in there more than fifty minutes now. He'd called to her several more times in the past few minutes but got no reply. Unable to ignore any longer the feeling that something was very wrong, he reached for the doorknob with a gloved hand and was taken aback to find that it wasn't locked. He opened the door a crack. Steam curled out through the opening, and the shower noise became several times louder.

'Hey! What's going on in here? I'm opening the door!'

No reply. He pushed the door wide and stepped into the bathroom. And as the steam began to dissipate, the girl materialised on the edge of the tub. She was sitting there completely nude, stabbing herself in the right thigh with the scissors of a Swiss Army knife. When she noticed Kawashima, she gave him a little smile and spread her legs as if to show him the bits of bloody flesh that had caught in her pubic hair. The wounds weren't very deep, but she had gouged a good deal of flesh from the thigh, and blood was pooled on the tile floor at her feet.

He instinctively moved to stop her, but at his first step the girl opened her mouth, drew a big breath, and let out a scream that rattled the mirror and chilled him to the bone. After a scream like that, someone might be pounding on the door any minute. He had to show the girl that he wasn't going to approach any closer. He stepped back into the doorway, and she immediately reverted to her vacant little smile.

If anyone were to search his bag they'd find the knife and the ice pick. Maybe he should call the girl's office. There was a telephone receiver on the wall right next to him, but it was for incoming calls only. He took another step back, and the expression on her face underwent an immediate change. Terror showed in her eyes and brow, and she opened her mouth wide and sucked in another big breath. She was going to scream again.

'I'm not going anywhere!' Kawashima said quickly. 'OK?' He leaned against the doorframe. 'Do you understand?'

She nodded, very slowly and almost imperceptibly.

I'll be damned, he thought. She's scared half to death. Just like the little kids back in the Home. She wants me here, but not too close. She panics if I approach, and she panics if I try to leave. Stabbing herself like that because she doesn't know any other way to ask for help.

The girl had been holding the knife down at her side since he'd appeared, but now she raised it and plunged the scissors into the blood-dark meat of her thigh again. It sounded like when you step in mud – *splut*. She didn't look at the scissors or the wound but kept her eyes on Kawashima. And just then the telephone rang, giving him such a jolt that his shoulder slid off the doorframe and he nearly fell down. The girl screwed up her face and laughed in a wet, throaty voice.

'Mr Yokoyama? Is everything all right, sir?'

The call was from the front desk. No doubt someone in a neighbouring room, or a security guard maybe, had reported the scream. Everything's fine, Kawashima said over the hammering of his heartbeat, trying desperately to sound calm.

'As you may be aware, sir, all our rooms are occupied tonight, and some of our guests are already sleeping, so we would very much appreciate it if you could keep the volume as low as possible when enjoying music or television.' The man went on to thank him for his cooperation and to bid him a formal and courteous good night.

What a roundabout way of complaining, Kawashima thought. Somewhere a little kid was getting his brains beaten to a pulp because he'd wet the bed; somewhere a woman who'd broken some arbitrary rule was being taken to a room where unspeakable things could be done to her away from prying eyes; and meanwhile: *Is everything all right, sir? Thank you so much for your cooperation, sir* – a complaint that sounded more like an apology.

'Who are you?' the girl growled in her wet voice. He leaned back against the doorframe and didn't answer. 'Who *are* you!'

He mustn't say anything. No matter what he said, she would merely shout him down and refuse to listen. She was like a wounded animal. Try to get close and she'd bare her fangs; try to leave and she'd yowl for help.

Kawashima held his right index finger up to his lips in a silent *Shhh*. He remembered the way he'd felt when he was first put in the Home, convinced that any adult who came up to him smiling and offering kindly words was the enemy. Right now they're making nice, he'd tell himself, but sooner or later they'll be pounding on me, for reasons I won't even understand. As a little boy, Kawashima had never been able to fathom what it was about himself that made adults so angry, but the thought of being completely abandoned by them was even scarier than the unpredictable attacks. All he'd learned for certain in his few years on earth was that he was powerless, incapable of surviving on his own, and that the people he came into contact with all seemed to despise him. He knew from his own experience that he mustn't approach this girl, and he mustn't leave her, and he mustn't speak directly to her or even answer her questions. She wants help, he thought, but she can't let down her guard. That's why she's staring at me like that, watching my every move.

When he put his finger to his lips, the girl studied the gesture curiously and let the knife dangle at her side again. Kawashima slowly took off his gloves and dropped them in the wastebasket next to the door.

He showed her his bare palms, as if to say: *Calm down. Calm down. I'm not going to hurt you.* As he did this, and without turning his head, he looked down at her open purse, which was sitting beside the sink. He could see cosmetics, a memo pad, and a small envelope of the sort hospitals dispense medicine in. Handwritten in ink beneath the gothic-style printing that said *Shiroyama Medical Clinic – Dr Shiroyama Yasuhiro, Director* was the name Sanada Chiaki.

He mustn't speak directly to her, even to answer a question, so he needed some sort of intermediary. He lifted the telephone receiver from the wall unit and held it to his ear, tucking his free hand underneath to surreptitiously hold down the hook. The last thing he needed was to connect to an emergency operator while pretending to speak on the phone.

'Hello?' he said. 'Yes, that's right. Sanada Chiaki is here with me now.'

He looked over his shoulder at the girl. The hand holding the knife still hung at her side, and she was watching him closely, trying to comprehend what was happening. The first order of business was to get that knife away from her.

'She still doesn't really trust me. I'm completely on her side, and I'd never do anything to hurt her, but she doesn't understand that yet.'

When the man first came into the bathroom, Chiaki

had felt her face light up with a smile. This must be *him*, she thought – the one who always takes me to the hospital. When she began stabbing herself in the thigh, she'd had, as usual, no idea who she was or where she was, and naturally she hadn't felt any pain. Unfolding the little scissors, she'd remembered wanting to do something fun with them but couldn't remember what. She knew what she was going to be doing, however. It was what she always had to do whenever that face appeared before her eyes, the face of You-know-who with his bright white shirt. She didn't know who she was. But she knew what her name was, because You-know-who kept whispering it in her face. *Chiaki*. My name is Chiaki. I'm someone they call Chiaki. He calls me that, and he's licking me down there, so there's no doubt about it – Chiaki is me.

But who was she? And *where* was she? That was the question, but the answer didn't really matter. What mattered was that she needed to be punished. And the one who knew she needed to be punished was the real her. Chiaki was just a name. There was nothing in it. *Chi-a-ki* – three empty little syllables. *Die*, said a voice. And it was her, the real her, moving her lips and using her voice to say the word. She was the one telling herself to die – that was all she could be sure of right now. *Die, why don't you? Why don't you just drop dead, Chiaki?*

How proud I'd be if I could actually kill her, she thought. Stab her in the thigh and hear the skin puncturing, like when you spear a sausage with a fork. But then things get hazier and hazier, and finally you wake up in the hospital. *Somebody* always takes me there. Kazuki said it was him who called the ambulance last time, but that was a lie. It's someone I've never met, and it definitely isn't You-know-who. All You-know-who ever did was lick me down there and suddenly start yelling at everybody. I've always wanted to meet him, the one who takes me to the hospital. I've always hoped to see his face just once, but I never really thought it would happen. He's somebody very special, a very important person. It's not so easy to meet people like that.

And yet, this man just might be him. That's what she'd thought when he opened the bathroom door, but of course there was no way to be sure. Maybe it's someone completely different, she cautioned herself. A bad person. Someone who hates me and wants to get rid of me. But she'd asked him who he was, and he hadn't answered. That was a good sign. A bad man would've made up some lie. At least she knew he wasn't a liar. And now he was saying her name to someone on the telephone. Who was he talking to? The hospital?

'Yes, Chiaki is here. She's hurt. I want to help her, but she still doesn't trust me. What? Is that so? All right, then, I'll put her on the phone.'

The man held the receiver out to her. Who could it be? She rose unsteadily to her feet, and all the blood that had collected in the wounds washed down her leg.

The moment the girl was within reach of the receiver, Kawashima made his move. He snatched hold of her right wrist with one hand and prised her fingers open with the other. The Swiss Army knife clattered to the floor. The girl stared blankly at the hand that held her wrist for some moments, as if unable to process what had just happened, and then, suddenly, she was twisting and thrashing and kicking. With a flick of his shoe, Kawashima sent the knife skittering over the tiles to the far corner of the bathroom. He then pivoted behind the girl and threw his arms around her wet body, pinning her own slender arms to her sides. She glared at him over her shoulder with wide, wild eyes, opened her mouth, and took a deep, wheezing in-breath.

Kawashima clamped his left hand over her mouth before she could scream. There was so little of her that he needed only his right arm to keep her more or less immobile. She was kicking his shins with her bare heels, but feebly, and he scarcely felt it. The problem was the hand on her mouth. Curling back her lips like a cornered dog, the girl bit into the base of his middle finger, where it met the palm. She was biting as hard as she could, squeezing her eyes shut and scrunching up her face, and her teeth broke the flesh and severed a nerve. A sickening chill shuddered through Kawashima's body, but he fought off the impulse to pull his hand away and began whispering in her ear:

'It's all right. It's all right, it's all right. I would never hurt you, I would never hurt you.'

This isn't my pain! he was shouting inwardly; but it wasn't working – his finger hurt like hell. He had to hand it to this girl. She was worthy of the ice pick, and she was going to get it as soon as she calmed down.

'Don't be angry,' he whispered gently. 'Don't be angry. Don't be angry, everything's all right. It's all right, OK? Everything's all right. You don't have to be afraid. There's nothing to be afraid of.'

The man's voice was deep and soft and nice, but he was holding her from behind, and all Chiaki could think was that someone was trying to take control of her. There was a coppery taste and the sticky texture of blood in her mouth. The voice in her ear saying 'Don't be angry' never varied in tone or volume. *Don't be angry, don't be angry. You don't have to be afraid.*

You don't have to be afraid. There's nothing to be afraid of. And slowly, as the words were repeated again and again, they began to sink in. It was true: she really was angry, and afraid of something. No one had ever pointed that out to her before. She decided it was all right to relax her guard and promptly wilted in the man's arms.

Kawashima carried the girl to the sofa and laid her limp body down. Her eyes were half-closed and bleary, her mouth open, her lips and teeth flecked with blood, her breathing faint and slow. He dried her with a bath towel and inspected the scissor wounds. The skin of her thigh was punctured in ten or more places, but the cuts weren't deep and some had already stopped bleeding. It's not too late to murder her, he thought. She was lying before him, perfectly still, and the knife and ice pick were right there under the sweatshirt in his open bag. He lightly touched one of her wounds, and she didn't react in any way. She's all numbed out, he thought. Stabbing someone in a state like this would be like stabbing a mannequin. She probably wouldn't even try to scream if he cut her Achilles tendons; she'd probably greet death with this same out-of-it expression on her face. And besides, he ruminated, balling a tissue in his left fist to stop his own bleeding . . .

Besides, she's one of us. A kindred spirit. Are you

going to stab a woman who's hacked her own leg into a bloody mess and who's lying there looking like death warmed over? Best to give up on the whole idea. The plan had gone completely awry. His suit was wet, and there was blood on the cuffs of his trousers. He'd taken off the gloves, his fingerprints were all over the place, and his left hand was gouged and bleeding. It would be impossible to hide the wound, and bits of his skin would be stuck to her teeth. No, he'd have to abort and start all over again from scratch.

He took off his shirt and used the knife to cut out a long strip of cloth. Doubling up a clean face towel, he placed it over the wounds on the girl's thigh, then wrapped the strip of cloth around it. He was fairly sure this would stop the bleeding. As he changed into the jeans and sweatshirt, he shook his head ruefully: he'd bought a combat knife with a blade as long as his forearm and ended up using it to slice through a cheap shirt instead of a pair of Achilles tendons. The girl's eyes were closed now, and her naked breast rose and fell slowly with her breathing, but he couldn't tell if she was actually asleep or not. He got a blanket from the closet and draped it over her.

After devising a smaller bandage for his left hand, Kawashima wrapped up the knife and the ice pick again. The bundles were fairly bulky, what with all the layers of cardboard and paper and duct tape, and surprisingly heavy. He had to dispose of them somewhere – the farther away the better, ideally, but these weren't ideal circumstances. Maybe he could just dump them in one of the trash receptacles near the elevator, though on a different floor of course. Then he'd call the S&M club and have them come get the girl. They probably wouldn't report anything to the hotel or to the police. But since there was no way to be sure of that, or of what sorts of characters they might send to retrieve her, it would be foolhardy to have weapons in the room. He didn't want to throw away the notes, though. They'd cost him a lot of time and effort, and the thought of starting all over again was daunting. Anyway, having notes was no crime. He'd be all right as long as the knife and ice pick weren't found in the room.

Checking to see that the girl's eyes were still closed, he picked up the vinyl bag containing the two bundles, slipped the room key into his pocket, and stepped out into the corridor. He closed the door behind him and stood there a moment, getting his bearings. Room 2902 was at the very end of the twenty-ninth floor. There was a certain surreal quality to the long corridor, and it took him some time to realise that the faint buzzing in his ears was in fact the sound of a TV somewhere. But merely stepping outside the room, away from the girl, had helped dissipate some of the tension – which perhaps explained why his finger was suddenly hurting like hell again. The gash was a deep one, and his tissue-paper and shirt-cloth bandage wasn't doing much to stop the flow of blood.

He was slowly making his way down the corridor when a door opened just ahead and an elderly couple emerged. They were speaking together in English and dressed as if they'd just returned from a round of golf. Kawashima was walking past with his head down, when the woman startled him by flashing a big smile and saying, 'Excuse me, sir!'

He felt as if both she and the man were eyeing the vinyl bag and the bandage on his hand, but apparently she was asking him about restaurants. Kawashima's English was shaky at best, but she seemed to be saying that they'd been told the restaurants in Tokyo hotels were outrageously expensive. Could he recommend a nice place nearby, preferably Italian or Continental? The husband protested that she should ask the front desk or concierge, that it was rude to bother a complete stranger with such things, and gestured for Kawashima to walk on and pay no attention to her, but he too was wearing a big smile. They reminded Kawashima of the sort of elderly couple you see in old American movies. He excused himself, ducking his head apologetically, and continued down the corridor towards the elevator, but of course the elderly pair were going that way too and walked along behind him, talking quietly. It would not be good to get on the elevator with these two, he thought. Getting off at any level other than the lobby or the restaurants would strike them as odd, and they might even remember which floor it was. If calling the S&M club should lead to any sort of complication, he couldn't risk having the ice pick and knife discovered and linked to him.

He stopped and pretended to search his pockets as if he'd forgotten something. As the couple passed him, he wished them a good evening and did an about-face to head back towards his room. And no sooner had he spun on his heel than he saw the door to room 2902 open and Sanada Chiaki come staggering out into the corridor, completely nude. Kawashima froze, and the vinyl bag nearly slipped from his hand. If he broke into a run, the elderly couple would hear his footsteps and turn to look. And what they would see was like a scene from a nightmare – a thin, naked, blood-smeared Japanese girl with a crude bandage wrapped around her thigh, stumbling down the corridor of their hotel. Glancing back at them, he saw that they hadn't yet noticed anything and were about to turn the corner to the elevator hall. The girl was slumped against the wall, looking around her in a bewildered way, as if wondering where she was and which way to run.

The moment the elderly couple disappeared around the corner, Kawashima broke into a sprint. He prayed that no other doors would open before he got to her.

When she saw the man running towards her Chiaki gave a little squeal. She turned to flee but ran into the wall, scraping her knee on the plaster and falling back on to her rear end. When Kawashima caught up to her she was scrambling to escape on all fours. He bent down to reach under her arms and drag her back to the room, but it was no easy job moving an unwilling woman – petite or not – even a few metres. Pinning her under his left arm, with the vinyl bag still dangling from that hand, he searched his right-hand pocket for the key. As the girl thrashed about, the bouncing bag dislodged his bandage and the wound at the base of his finger began bleeding freely again. He somehow managed to get the key in the lock and to open the door, and just as he tumbled inside with the girl, throwing her to the carpet as if tackling her, he heard another door closing somewhere down the corridor. The pain in his left hand was intense, and his heart felt as if it were going to explode.

Had someone seen them? In any case, he certainly couldn't call the S&M club now. He hadn't even disposed of the weapons yet. The girl lay in the entry-way, moaning.

'*Owww!* It *hurrrts!*'

Minutes earlier, awaking from the briefest of naps, Chiaki had found herself back in touch with all five senses, and the pain had been excruciating. Her thigh was clumsily wrapped with a makeshift bandage, and when she stood up a rivulet of blood ran down her leg to the top of her foot. She was scared. She'd have to go to the hospital again. The man who always took her there had been at her side just a moment ago – she could still feel the warmth of his arms around her. Her teeth were coated with a sticky substance, and her tongue discovered something like a bit of rubber band stuck to her upper gum. She fished this out and looked at it. It had a pattern of little grooves, and when she realised it was a piece of human skin, she remembered having bitten the man's finger. She could still hear the way he'd whispered in her ear: *It's all right, don't be angry, there's nothing to be afraid of.* To think that even as he was whispering things like that in her ear, she was tearing his flesh with her teeth . . . She limped to the bathroom, groaning with each step, but the man wasn't in there either. She picked up the navy-blue suit he'd been wearing and shook it out, waving it in the air and shouting, 'Where *are* you?' Spotting his overnight bag next to the desk, she snatched it up and threw it against the wall, then hobbled to the door. Only after she'd stepped out into the corridor did she realise she wasn't wearing any clothes. The door slowly swung closed behind her, and it had just dawned on her that she couldn't get back inside when she saw the man running towards her from way down the corridor. But wait. This couldn't be the same man – he was wearing different clothes. Terrified at this realisation, she'd scrambled to get away, but the man had caught her and dragged her back into the room. Once inside, she noticed the wound on his hand and thought: It's him after all.

'Listen to me!' Kawashima said, gasping for breath. 'Can you, understand, what I'm saying?'

Chiaki nodded, staring at his face and trying to fix it in her memory. Of course I understand what you're saying, she thought. You want to take me to the hospital, right?

'First of all, would you, please, put your clothes on?'

He had to get out of this hotel as soon as possible. Someone may have seen them just now, and he still had the knife and ice pick in his possession. He should probably take her to a hospital. Escort her to an emergency room, get her some treatment, and the S&M club could have no cause for complaint. He was the one who was being inconvenienced here, after all. Surely they'd be satisfied if he explained things properly and paid for six hours of her time.

'Please? Please get dressed.'

He'd throw everything into his bag and check out immediately. The fact that he was with a woman would make an impression on the clerk, but he couldn't worry about that at this point. I haven't actually done anything anyway, he told himself. Get in a taxi, take her to the nearest hospital, and wash my hands of the whole thing.

'We're going to the hospital. You can't very well go naked, right?'

Chiaki was ecstatic. So it really was him. The one who'd grabbed her from behind and whispered in her ear and made her realise how angry and scared she was, was the same one who always saw to it that she got to a hospital. It's really him, she thought. I've finally met the mystery man.

'OK,' she said, peering at his face and nodding. 'But let me call my office first, OK?'

She limped to the telephone on the table, and Kawashima went into the bathroom to gather her things. The Swiss Army knife was on the floor. He used a tissue to pick it up, wiped the blood from the scissors, folded them back into the handle, and dropped the knife into her purse. He'd left the door open so he could hear her talking on the phone.

'That's right, I'm not feeling well so I'm going to finish up now, but it's all right if I don't come by the office, isn't it? It's, let's see, just after ten, so . . . four hours, right? Don't worry, I'll go to the hospital if it keeps getting worse.'

Kawashima heard her hang up and turned on the shower to wash the remaining blood from the bath-tub and floor. Even the blood that had already dried cleaned up nicely with a wet towel. *I'm not feeling well and might have to go to the hospital* – couldn't have invented a better story myself, he thought with some relief. He carried the girl's purse and under-garments and dress into the bedroom. She was sitting on the sofa, still naked except for that silvery ring in her nipple.

'Can you help me with my panties?' She lifted her legs so that her toes pointed at him. 'I'm afraid I'll hurt my leg.'

He knelt before her with the rolled-up panties in both hands, slipped them over her feet and pushed them up her shins to her knees, then let go and told her to stand. She put a hand on his shoulder and rose unsteadily to her feet, her thin pubic hair nearly brushing against his face. Stretching the elastic as far as it would go, he managed to pull the panties up without disturbing the bandage, then unrolled the purple, translucent material to snugly encase her crotch and buttocks.

'I don't need to put on my stockings, right? They'll just make me take them off again, right?'

Kawashima grunted agreement and stood up. It was then that he noticed his overnight bag lying on its side against the opposite wall, and his open notebook beside it. His blood turned to ice. She must have read the notes, he thought, and a shiver emanating from his bitten finger rippled through every cell in his body. He experienced a surge of nausea and looked over at the girl, who had turned her back to him and was climbing into her slip. I have no choice now, he thought, and the chill and the nausea merged with a peculiar, bubbling excitement. I have no choice but to kill her. If she read the notes and lived, there couldn't be a next time. She'd be sure to tell someone: *I had a client like that once.*

It was a good thing he hadn't disposed of the ice pick and combat knife after all.

He had to walk slowly to keep from outpacing the girl, who was limping along beside him, holding his arm. Wind whistled through the canyon of skyscrapers, and on the empty street the cold seemed to seep into every pore. For a moment he even forgot about the pain in his finger.

'It's *freezing*,' the girl said, turning up the collar of

her coat, hunching her back and clinging even more tightly to his arm.

What a strange woman, he thought – why's she so thrilled about going to the hospital? Well, at least she hadn't caused any problems when he was checking out. She'd clung to his arm like this in the elevator too, but when they reached the lobby she let go and headed straight for the exit without so much as a backward glance, as if they had nothing to do with each other. Probably second nature for a girl in her profession, but he was glad not to have been seen leaving the hotel with her.

Chiaki hadn't wanted to let go of the man's arm in the lobby, but she guessed he wouldn't care to be seen cuddling with her in front of a lot of people. Nobody likes to be seen with me in public, she thought. Even Mama, after I told her what You-know-who was doing, started walking a few steps ahead when we went out together. That's me: a woman other people are ashamed to be seen with.

Waiting for his receipt at the checkout counter, Kawashima had peered over the rim of his fake glasses to watch her crossing the lobby. She slumped along with bent head and rounded shoulders, dangling her sizeable bag of toys from one hand and her purse from the other.

*

'Emergency room of the nearest hospital, please,' Kawashima said, and the driver asked if Sogo Hospital in Yoyogi would be all right. Kawashima didn't care which hospital it was, and neither did the girl. It was warm inside the taxi, but she snuggled up to him anyway, twisting her upper body to bury her face in his chest. There had been girls like this in the Home, Kawashima remembered. He knew she wasn't doing this because she liked him, that any moment her attitude could change completely. You never knew what someone like this might do. She might laugh hysterically out of sheer terror, only to end up sobbing and attacking you with her fists. She might be all over you one minute and act as if you didn't exist the next.

In other words, her clinging to him like this was by no means an indication that she hadn't read the notes. He'd have to spend more time with her before he'd know for sure.

'Emergency room, eh?' the driver said, glancing in the rear-view mirror. 'Anything wrong?'

The girl laughed in a weird voice – a voice remarkably like the beeping of an ATM – and said, 'I'm having a baby.'

Kawashima shook his head. What an imbecilic thing to say. The driver had seen her standing at the kerb, and would surely have noticed how slender she was. You could have encircled her waist with two hands.

'Aren't I?' she said, looking up at Kawashima.

He didn't bother to reply. He glanced at her moist eyes for a moment, but the expression on his face gave her nothing.

'You look good with those glasses on,' she said.

He stared straight ahead, thinking: Hurry up and get us to the hospital.

'Your eyes are really pretty through the lenses.'

Chiaki had begun to sense that this man, her mystery man, was in fact very wealthy. He was so calm and dignified, and really kind of handsome up close. And somehow she knew she could trust him completely. Normally, whenever she said something she really believed, something straight from the heart, or made a clever joke, all she'd get from people were phony reactions. But this man wasn't saying anything or reacting at all, so she knew he wasn't a phony, or a liar. He'd been wearing that cheap suit at first, and the things he had on now – the coat, the sweatshirt and jeans, the shoes, even the glasses – were chintzy too, but maybe he was in disguise. Maybe he'd disguised himself because he was embarrassed about the whole idea of S&M. He'd reserved her for six hours but never even touched her in a sexual way. And he'd paid her for six even though she said she'd only charge him for four. He was nothing like all her other clients – *Hurry up and take it off, hurry up and show it to me, hurry up and lick it, hurry up and suck it* – he was different, in every way. And even though her leg had been hurting really bad, she'd got wet when he put her panties on for her. He must've gone to that hotel incognito for one night of fun, she thought, just to try something new. I bet he's from Kyoto or Kobe, someplace like that. And I bet he's even got another room at a different hotel, probably some unbelievable luxury suite.

'Hey,' she said softly, smiling up at him. 'What hotel are you staying at really?'

Kawashima's body stiffened.

I knew it, Chiaki said to herself – he's a secret rich man.

Sure enough, thought Kawashima – she read the notes.

Most of the hospital's windows were dark. The driver dropped them off at the side entrance and watched them move slowly, arm in arm, up the walkway to the door.

'Listen, I'll be waiting right here,' Kawashima told the girl. 'I don't want to go in, but I won't move from this spot. I don't like hospitals, never did. I mean, the truth is, I'm afraid of them. Hospitals scare me.'

His breath made little clouds as he spoke. They were standing in front of a lighted sign that said

EMERGENCY OUTPATIENT RECEPTION. The reception room would be brightly lit, and he couldn't afford to be seen with the girl in a place like that, especially by any doctors or nurses.

'OK,' said Chiaki, thinking: So that's why he's never around when I wake up – he doesn't like hospitals. 'But shouldn't you have them look at your hand?'

'I'll be all right,' Kawashima said. He took three 10,000-yen notes from his pocket and held them out to her. 'Use this to pay.'

'That's OK,' said the girl, shaking her head. 'You already paid me extra and everything.' She stepped towards the door beneath the sign, then stopped and looked back at him. 'You'll be right here, right?'

'I promise.'

'And you'll stay with me tonight, won't you?'

'Of course. I won't leave you.'

I've got to snuff her as soon as possible and get this over with, Kawashima thought as he watched her enter the building. The longer I put it off, the greater the risk that someone will get a good look at us together.

Chiaki shook her head when the nurse asked if she had her insurance card, and she had to present her driver's licence and write her name and address on some forms. When she got in to see the doctor she told him she'd fallen off a bicycle. He inspected the wounds on her thigh and said that one of them was fairly deep and would require stitches. He didn't question her story or ask about the shirt-cloth bandage, and though he must have seen the scars from all the previous incidents he didn't say anything about them either. He injected her with a local anaesthetic in three different spots, disinfected the scraped knee and the wounds and sewed up the deep one, and covered them all with lots of gauze. He seemed to be in a hurry to finish.

There had been about ten other people in the waiting room. A man with a shaved head sitting in a wheelchair, his eyes half-closed and his mouth hanging open, wearing just a thin cotton robe; a middle-aged woman with thick make-up whose big toe and ankle were swollen grotesquely, and who was supported by two thin young men sitting on either side of her; a group of four men dressed for construction work who smelled of sweat and sat with their heads bent together, discussing something in low voices; an old man with bulging purple veins on his hands reading a newspaper; a man cradling a baby, next to a woman holding a stuffed toy chipmunk and pressing a handkerchief to her eyes.

The anaesthetic had taken effect in just a few minutes, but Chiaki still felt a little pain when the suturing needle pierced her flesh, and beads of sweat broke out on her upper lip and the bridge of her nose. Each time the doctor's arm brushed against her translucent purple panties she thought of the man with the glasses on, the way his eyes looked behind those lenses.

'Is it OK to have sex?' she asked as she was leaving the examination room. Without even glancing up from the chart he was scribbling on, the doctor muttered, 'Just be careful the bandage doesn't come off.'

Kawashima had taken refuge across the street from the entrance, at a bus stop with partitions to protect him from the freezing wind. He'd decided that loitering outside an emergency room entrance at eleven o'clock on a cold night like this, holding two large bags, just wouldn't look right. If a cop on patrol were to come along and question him and then ask to look in the bags, he'd find the girl's S&M toys in one and an ice pick and combat knife in the other. At a bus stop, on the other hand, there was nothing suspicious about carrying luggage of any size. He had a clear view of the hospital doors from here, and if a bus were to come he had only to act as if he were waiting for a different one.

His clothes – T-shirt, sweatshirt, and jeans under a cheap coat of thin material – were no match for this weather, though. He'd finally stopped bleeding, but his fingers were frozen, and he reopened the wound by putting his leather gloves back on. He wondered if he couldn't separate himself from the cold and the pain, using the technique he'd developed as a boy. There were a lot of things he had to think through right now, while the girl was receiving treatment, but conditions like this robbed you of the power to process information. The technique . . .

It had been a cold night in winter, just like this, when he first discovered it. He'd run out of the house and slammed the sliding glass door behind him. Come to think of it, the palm of his left hand was hurting that night, too. Mother had coated it with industrial ammonia – the kind you dilute ten parts to one to use as insecticide. In a little while it had begun to make this awful smell, and he felt the skin of his palm burning. When he tried to wash the stuff off she pulled him away from the sink, and he ran outside. *Don't bother coming back!* she shouted through the glass and locked the door, turning the latch slowly, deliberately. *Clack*. Her silhouette on the frosted glass was terrifying, blurry at the edges and bigger than life, and he was freezing and in so much pain that he thought he was going to lose his mind. I must've made use of that, he thought, that feeling that I was going insane. Something came flooding into me, I remember, and something went flooding out, and suddenly I'd managed to separate myself from the pain and the cold and the fear.

The one who's here right now isn't me. This pain isn't mine. That was the general idea, but of course he hadn't put it into words at the time. The words had all been erased, along with the feelings. He'd used the technique later on in life, too, when he lived with the stripper. He seemed to remember subtly shifting the focus of his eyes, like with one of those 3-D illustrations, but there was no way he could maintain that sort of concentration right now. And it was no use trying to analyse how he'd done it. The instant you put something like that into words, it was gone. Words and combinations of words – the more you relied on them, the less power you actually had.

About two hundred metres from the bus stop was a phone booth. If only he were inside it. He'd be completely protected from the wind, and he could even call Yoko and hear her voice if he wanted to. He was summoning up the sound of that soothing voice of hers when, absurdly, he began to imagine actually asking her advice.

'So, anyway, she read the notes. I have no choice but to kill her, right? What else can I do?'

'Where is she right now?'

'She's in the emergency room at this hospital. I'm outside waiting for her.'

'Won't she say something to the doctor, or one of the nurses?'

'I don't think so.'

'Why not?'

'Well, if she was going to do that, she could've talked to someone in the lobby of the hotel, right? The security guard or whatever.'

'I guess that's true. But if she read the notes, why isn't she trying to escape?'

'I don't get that part, either, but it's not as if this is a woman who's in control of herself, or acting rationally. I'm pretty sure she's a kindred spirit.'

'Kindred spirit?'

'I think something happened to her when she was small.'

'Like what?'

'I don't know, and I don't want to know, but I can tell she's afraid, and starved for something.'

'So, what are you going to do now?'

A slender figure came out through the emergency room door. She was hopping on one leg and looking anxiously about. *One thing's for sure*, Kawashima muttered under his breath as he sprinted towards the girl. *I can't take her back to the hotel in Akasaka.*

He really did wait for me, Chiaki thought when

she saw the man running to her out of the frozen darkness. She thought he looked like a steam locomotive in an old cartoon, lugging those two big bags and expelling clouds of white smoke. And it was comical the way he dangled her Lancel bag from the crook of his left arm, like a lady. Of course he can't hold it in his hand because of his finger, she thought – but just look at him, running like that for all he's worth. How cute can you get?

Not wanting to wait a single extra second to feel his arm around her shoulder, supporting her, Chiaki started towards the man, dragging her numb, anaesthetised right leg.

'Come to my place,' she said as they settled into a taxi. 'You'll come and stay with me, won't you?'

Kawashima's lips and cheeks were stiff with the cold, and he merely nodded rather than trying to speak. Her place would certainly work for him. He couldn't take her to the hotel in Akasaka, where he was registered under his real name, and had been thinking he might have to make do with a love hotel after all.

Chiaki never thought to question the man's motivation for accompanying her to the hospital – or for waiting outside, for that matter. She had long since lost sight of the fact that he was merely a client who'd happened to call her club and ask for a girl to be sent to his hotel room. All she could see were his selfless efforts on her behalf, which, in her mind at least, were beginning to take on epic proportions.

He stood out there in this freezing weather waiting for me, she thought. His arm felt like *ice* – I never even knew a body could *get* that cold. I was afraid he wouldn't really wait for me, and when he wasn't right outside the door I almost fainted, but then there he was, humping it across the street as fast as he could go, huffing and puffing clouds of steam. It was like being in a movie, like being lead actress in some big romantic scene.

It was warm inside the taxi, but the man was still shivering. His face, just above and to the right of hers, looked distorted, the features out of balance. It was as if only some of his facial muscles had thawed while the rest remained frozen solid. His hair, exposed all that time to the cold wind, was dry and mussed, his teeth were chattering, and his nose was runny. His eyes were watering, too, and he kept blinking. His face was a complete mess, in fact, and yet it was also the most adorable thing she'd ever seen. She had a sudden urge to hit that face. Not just give him a little slap on the cheek but slug him as hard as she could, with her fist or a bottle or a wrench or something, right in the eye. He'd be bleeding and begging her to stop, and she'd just laugh. He'd be even cuter weeping and asking for forgiveness, she thought. And after that he'd stay by her side for ever, no matter what.

Chiaki wanted to communicate these feelings to him. How nice it would be if she could tell him everything, even all the bad stuff. She could see herself tugging on his sleeve, going: *Listen, listen, I know you probably don't like to hear about things like this? But I really really hate my father. I do. Everybody thinks he's a good man, a nice, respectable gentleman, and he was head accountant for the biggest company in our home town and didn't even have any interests or hobbies outside of work except for spending like an hour every day feeding the goldfish, but from about the time I started elementary school, whenever my mother was away or after she'd gone to sleep, he'd do nasty things to me. He really did. That's why I've always just wished he would hurry up and die, and he's told me to drop dead too, lots of times. I really and truly wish he would die, but when I was in middle school my tonsils kept getting inflamed and finally I got a really bad fever and they decided to take them out? And we lived in this small town outside Nagoya that didn't even have a real hospital, so our local doctor was going to perform the operation, and at the dinner table my mother was worrying about that, saying she wondered if the doctor really knew what*

*he was doing, and my father said, 'If anything happens
to Chiaki I'll kill that son of a bitch,' and then he
burst into tears. I mean, I was amazed. At the time
our family was a shambles because I'd finally told my
mother what he was doing to me, and after that he
turned into this really mean and angry person who
was always yelling, but him saying that about the
doctor and crying, that's the thing I remember most.
You don't see a grown man cry very often, right? I
changed my personality too, right after I entered
junior college, except I did it on purpose, and after
that boys started liking me more, and I have three
boyfriends right now, sort of, but don't be jealous,
OK? You don't have anything to be jealous about.
They're all losers, really. One's named Kazuki; he's a
college student, but in high school he crashed his
motorcycle, and his shoulder and knee are messed up,
and he's always saying he wants to die. I like to watch
boys when they're sleeping really soundly? So about
six months ago I crushed up three Halcion tablets and
mixed them in Kazuki's Campari and orange, and ever
since then he won't eat or drink anything I give him.
They're all like that. Yoshiaki's this guy who when I
tried to stab myself in the leg he got all hysterical,
and then when I pricked him just a little with the
knife he ran away. He's twenty-eight now but he's still
just a clerk in a video store. Atsushi is young, the*

same age as me, and he just became a hairdresser, and he's half-white but near-sighted and doesn't have any parents. He's an orphan. He's always going on and on about his childhood, and when he gets drunk he might tell me he's going to kill me or he might start bawling like a baby, and sometimes he calls me Mommy. Atsushi's the one who taught me about piercings. He's got five rings in his ear, eighteen gauge to ten gauge, but when I told him to get one in his nipple to match mine, and to get a Sailor Moon *tattoo – because I like* Sailor Moon*? – or if not that, a skull, he stopped calling me. I was eighteen when I changed my personality, and in the three years since then I've had about twenty boyfriends, but they were all more or less like that. So you can understand how happy I am to finally meet someone like you!*

'Are you hungry?' she said.

The man nodded without taking his eyes off the road ahead and without any change of expression. High-rise buildings loomed on all sides, and the lights from the windows – so many different colours and shades – seemed to swirl around them, enveloping the two of them in a warm cocoon.

I can't communicate the way I feel to him, she thought, but I probably don't need to anyway. He's not going to ask me a lot of questions, and he's not going to tell me about himself. You can tell he doesn't like hearing or making confessions. Who knew there were still people like that in this world, though? Everybody wants to talk about themselves, and everybody wants to hear everybody else's story, so we take turns playing reporter and celebrity. *It must have made you very sad when your own father raped you – can you describe some of your feelings at the time? Yes, I wept and wept, wondering why something like this had to happen to* me. It's like that. Everyone's running around comparing wounds, like bodybuilders showing off their muscles. And what's really unbelievable is that they really believe they can heal the wounds like that, just by putting them on display.

This man was different. But she had to ask herself: Was he really the one she'd been waiting for? And her various selves – the self whose father licks her down there, the self who whispers *I love you* to him as he laps at her private parts, the self who watches from the corner of the ceiling, the self who commands her to die, the self who unfolds the scissors from the handle of the Swiss Army knife – all gave her the same reply: *Who knows?* How could anyone know what sort of man she was really waiting for? Up until now, she'd simply accepted whoever showed interest in her and put up with her and sacrificed for her and wanted her body.

Well, it doesn't matter if he's the one or not, Chiaki

thought and looked at the man, who wasn't even bothering to wipe his fogged-up lenses. Once we're in my room, I'll have him shedding tears of joy and gratitude.

'We're almost there,' she said. 'I'll make you some hot soup, or a nice stew or something, OK?'

'Ah,' Kawashima said in a hoarse whisper. Could he get to her room without being seen by anyone? All he knew for sure was that he needed to rest awhile. He'd rest first, and then plan the next move.

'Try these slippers; they're more for summer really, but they're nice, aren't they? They're from Morocco. I have lots of other kinds, too. See these? Antique Chinese – isn't the silk beautiful? Of course, they were for bound feet, so they're just to look at, you can't really wear them. The Moroccan ones feel a little rough if you're not wearing socks, but with socks on they're really comfortable, don't you think?'

It was a spacious one-room apartment with thick carpeting everywhere except the entryway and kitchenette. A big climate-control system built into one wall emitted heat with a low, almost inaudible hum. Next to this was a sliding glass door that led to a veranda with deckchairs. The skyscrapers of West Shinjuku were visible in the distance.

The taxi had dropped them off here, a small new

apartment complex midway between the shopping and residential districts of Shin-Okubo. There was no security guard in the lobby. The building was U-shaped, and in the centre was a cramped little garden with potted plants and an angel statue. The walls of the elevator were glass, so that you looked down at the angel falling away as you rose.

They'd got off at the sixth floor. In the corridor they passed an elderly man with a puppy, but the girl didn't say anything to him and he scarcely seemed to know they were there. The corridor was fairly dim, with soft indirect lighting, and Kawashima was sure the old man hadn't got much of a look at him.

The girl had slid an electronic key card into a slot and opened the door, then switched on a muted spotlight and introduced him to her slipper collection, which she kept on a rack in the entryway. He stepped into the Moroccan slippers she'd set out for him. They were yellow and looked like sandals.

'Would you like some espresso?' she asked. 'Or would you rather have a beer or gin and tonic or something like that?'

Kawashima opted for the caffeine, and the girl pointed out her espresso machine ('It's from Germany!') and took a Ginori demitasse cup from the cupboard. The machine was a professional model about the size of a large microwave oven, its stainless-steel housing and fixtures polished to a shine. She fiddled with it, then crossed the room to the closet beside her bed, where she hung up Kawashima's coat and began to undress. She was facing him when she squirmed out of her slip and let it fall to the floor. He studied her standing there in her purple panties and marvelled at how different a woman can look in different settings. He'd gazed at and grappled with this girl's naked body in the hotel room, the bathroom, and the corridor, but now somehow her skin seemed even whiter, almost luminous. And when he'd helped her into her panties he hadn't noticed the wisp of downy hair curling above the waistband towards her navel. What a beautiful tummy, he thought.

She put on a grey T-shirt and a loose-fitting brown velvet skirt that wouldn't constrict her bandaged wound. As she fastened the skirt, she looked over at Kawashima and mouthed the words *Just for now!* Meaning, he gathered, that she'd take it off again later.

'Nice room,' he said.

Thick, dark coffee began to trickle from the espresso machine into the fancy cup.

'I don't spend much money on anything else,' the girl said, walking to the kitchenette. She retrieved the cup, set it on the coffee table, and took a seat on the sofa beside him. 'A lot of girls like to go out drinking or clubbing or whatever? But I don't, and I don't buy that many clothes, either. I prefer to build my wardrobe little by little, you know what I mean? Just buying the things I really really like?'

Against the wall opposite the L-shaped sofa were the A/V rack and a bookshelf. There were paperback mysteries and horror novels, complete multi-volume sets of various girls' manga, and a photograph collection entitled *Corpses* mixed in with a number of oversize books about tableware and furniture. She had only a smattering of videos and CDs: three domestic animated films that had been big hits, a few CDs of the 'Greatest Classical Melodies' sort, and ten or twelve others that were movie soundtracks or 'best of' collections by Japanese pop stars. The TV screen was on the small side, and the stereo was just your average mini hifi system.

'After we rest a minute I'll make some soup,' Chiaki said. 'Would you like to listen to a little music?'

The man nodded, and she slid *Afternoon Classics, Volume III* into the CD player. It was the one with Chopin's *Nocturnes*, Schumann's *Scenes from Childhood*, and Schubert's *Moments Musicales*. She turned the volume low and sat back down even closer to the man, who'd already finished his espresso. She was about to say, *Doesn't the piano sound like rain?* – but he spoke first.

'It was too cold even to talk earlier,' Kawashima

said. As his body warmed in the heated room, that vision of the girl's white belly kept replaying in his mind, and he was suddenly excited again, and nervous. 'So, anyway, how did it go in the hospital?'

She lifted the hem of her velvet skirt and showed him the clean new bandage on her thigh. Kawashima wished he knew what she and the doctor had talked about. There was no guarantee she hadn't told him about the notes. For all he knew, the police, tipped off by the doctor, might already be staking out this apartment and stationing men outside the door, ready to burst in on them the moment the ice-pick made its appearance. But he hadn't noticed any cars tailing the taxi or any indications inside or outside the building that they were being watched. Well, he had time now to wait and feel things out. Surely he couldn't be arrested just for having an ice pick, a knife, and some notes on how to commit a murder. And if the girl were to lie and say he was the one who'd stabbed her in the thigh, all the police would have to do is inspect the wounds to see that they hadn't been made with an ice-pick or combat knife but with the tiny blades of her own Swiss Army scissors. And the depth and angle of the cuts would prove they'd been self-inflicted.

He was still gazing at the girl's new bandage when he became aware of a voice reverberating inside him, and a shiver vibrated out from his core. *Who are you kidding?* the voice said. *All you really care about is stabbing this girl with your ice pick.* It was the same voice he'd heard several days before, by the diaper shelf in the convenience store. *You still don't get it, do you? Can't you see that it isn't about maybe she saw the notes, or maybe she told someone? And that it doesn't even have anything to do with your fear of stabbing the baby? None of that really matters to you. Ask yourself this: Why did you come tagging along with this woman – to sit there snuggled up on the sofa drinking coffee? I don't think so. You did it because you're afraid of losing her. Why? You know perfectly well why. You were staring at her little white stomach when she changed clothes, weren't you? That pretty tummy with the soft brown peachfuzz. And you were thinking how you'd like to slowly open a small hole in that tummy with the point of an ice pick. That's all it's about for you. It's more important to you than anything else. To pull the ice pick back out and watch the thick, red blood ooze from that little hole. Your whole life has been leading up to this moment, when you reveal to the world the sort of human being you are. This is your debut as the real you. And guess who you have to thank for this opportunity?*

Mother? Kawashima detected an odour like hair or

fingernails burning. A fever was gathering between his temples. Sparks burst where his olfactory and optical and auditory nerves crossed and short-circuited, and his lips were trembling. He touched the nape of his neck. It was wet with perspiration, and he could feel his vocal cords were preparing to scream, all on their own. A scream of horror or exultation? He wasn't sure. He bit his lip, squeezed his eyes shut, and tore off the gloves he'd been wearing all this time, beginning with the left one. The newly formed scab had stuck to the inner lining; it peeled off, and he could feel fresh, warm blood seeping out again. He bowed his head and clenched the hand in a tight fist, trying to use the pain to gain control of himself.

'Oh, I forgot!' the girl said. 'We have to put something on that finger!'

Kawashima shook his head.

'But you have to disinfect it! I got some medicine from the doctor – I'll put some on for you, OK?'

He shook his head again. His eyes were still shut. He was barely listening to what the girl said, but something about the tenor of her voice was triggering a memory. It was like a voice he used to hear back in the Home whenever he had an episode. He'd be lost in his mind, no longer in control of himself, terrorised by the overpowering sense that something was about to burst or rip apart, the fever building between his temples, sparks flying where the sights and sounds and smells short-circuited, and then he'd hear this voice – an actual voice, coming not from within but from somewhere outside himself. It wasn't a scolding or appeasing or soothing voice, just matter-of-fact and real. *Masayuki, hey, it's dinner time. We're having everyone's favourite today – hamburgers! Time to wash up. Let's go and wash our hands. I know the water's cold, but we want those hands to be really clean! Everybody's happy because we're having hamburgers. See? See how happy they all are?* That voice would smother the sparks one by one and slowly cool the fever. *Take your fingers out of your ears now and open your eyes. Look around, listen to all the children talking and laughing. Everything's the same as ever. Nothing has changed, and no one is going to hurt you.*

Kawashima exhaled deeply, unclenching his left hand and opening his eyes. Keeping them closed was no more defence against the images that accompanied the sparks than plugging his ears was against the voice from inside, the voice he heard echoing off the interior walls of his skin. Only voices and images from the external world could neutralise those from inside. That was why Kawashima's greatest fear – far greater for him than the fear of death – was of losing his sight and hearing to some illness or accident. Cut off from actual sights and sounds, with the unchecked terror swelling inside him, he knew he'd go mad in no time. He looked at the girl, hoping she'd keep on talking.

'Oh, that's right,' she said. 'You're hungry, aren't you! I make really good soup. I mean, it's just instant, but instant can be delicious if you know what to add.'

Chiaki was wondering what was wrong with the man. Had she offended him? She couldn't think how. All she'd done was show him her new bandage, but he'd suddenly clammed up and closed his eyes and gone all pale in the face. The climate-control system kept the room at a pleasant temperature, but he was shivering. And he didn't seem to notice that he'd been biting his lip so hard he'd left a mark and even drawn a little blood.

'Like tonight, for example? I'm thinking I'll use a package of cream consommé. Knorr makes a good one, but on a cold night like this, when you feel chilled to the bone, potage is better than consommé, don't you think? You want something thick and hearty, right? So what I do is, I add a little curry powder, and milk of course, regular milk and also condensed milk, because it complements the sweetness of the corn? And besides, it's more nutritious that way, right?'

Chiaki was glad to see that as she chattered away

the man seemed to be listening closely, although there was something strangely vacant about the way he was nodding his head, focusing now on her bandaged thigh, now on her lips. The bandage must remind him of something, she thought. He's probably thinking about what I did in his bathroom at the hotel.

Of course. What else could it be?

She knew she'd been bad, but what exactly had she done? Chiaki was never conscious of any pain when she was hurting herself, and never had much memory of the incidents afterwards. All she could recall of the incident earlier this evening were fragmentary images, but she decided to see if she could patch them together. She'd never tried that before, and didn't really want to now but would do it for his sake. She remembered the way her thigh had looked, all chopped up and covered with blood. Now she had to retrieve the image of the man reacting to that. She concentrated on bringing the image into focus, and a field of little coloured dots of light separated and swirled and came back together and slowly began to set, like gelatine. The first image to resolve itself was the man standing by the bathroom door.

The door opens. The door opens. The bathroom door opens and this man is there. He's standing there. Just standing there. And his face? His face looks . . . scared. He looks so shocked, in fact, so *horrified*, that

I can hardly keep from laughing. That must be it. He caught me being bad in the bathroom, and it scared him so much that just to think about it now makes the blood drain from his face.

'I have two soup bowls I just bought,' she said. 'They're Wedgwood, and I haven't even tried them out yet. Don't worry, it won't take any time at all to make. I mean, all I have to do is boil the water and cut open the package and pour it in, and then basically just stir in the curry and milk.'

He got scared. Only natural, if you thought about it. After all, she'd been stabbing herself in the leg, right in front of him. How could she have forgotten that horrified look on his face, though? It must be because he didn't run away, she decided. Yoshiaki had run away, and the guy she was seeing in junior college, Yutaka – he went off saying he was going to call an ambulance and never came back. Hisao tried to stop her and got a cut on his hand, and sure enough he left too. They all ran away. That was why whenever she woke up in the hospital she let herself fantasise that some mystery man had taken her there.

She knew it was just a fantasy, just something her mind had dreamed up. There never had been any such man, not really. There were lots of different men instead, men in white clothes and white helmets who would catch hold of her and give her a shot in the arm and load her into a white van. That was the reality. She knew the mystery man wasn't real . . . and yet she couldn't help but wonder now. It just might be him, she thought. Because he didn't run away, even though he was horrified. And even though I bit his hand he just kept whispering gentle words in my ear.

No one had ever treated her like that before.

There was something else, too, something important that she couldn't quite recall. Another reason she'd thought he must be the mystery man. What was it? She reviewed the images from the bathroom one by one: the man's horrified face, his gestures, his hands, his arms. What was she forgetting? It was something in the bathroom. Bath towels, soap, shampoo, handbag, blood on the floor, wastebasket, box of tissues, bidet, toilet, toilet paper . . . Got it. The telephone.

'Adding curry powder to soup is a different idea, don't you think? Did you know that milk and curry go really well together? And sometimes they put corn in curry, right? You don't want to use any meat or anything. But if you put in a little curry powder – just a little – it accentuates the sweetness of the corn and the milk. I bet you didn't know that!'

He'd used the telephone in the bathroom. But the image of him standing there with his arms crossed, holding the phone, wasn't the important thing. The important thing was what he was saying. And when she remembered what that was, she felt goose bumps rising on the insides of her arms.

He said my name. *I'm with Chiaki right now*, that's what he said, my real name. That's what made me think he knew all about me. It must be him after all. And he probably does know all about me, too. I bet he's been watching me from afar. He didn't know how to approach me, so he pretended to be a client and asked the office to send me to him, and then all that stuff happened and he was scared but even so he didn't run away but stayed and helped me. That's why it didn't turn him on when I masturbated for him. He doesn't like me doing things like that. I hated it when he asked me right at the beginning if I'd take off my clothes and let him tie me up, but he didn't mean it, he wasn't going to do any such thing to me. If he were just another S&M freak he wouldn't have taken me to the hospital, and he never would have waited for me out in the freezing cold.

'Tell the truth,' she said, smiling at him.

Kawashima's heartbeat quickened at her sudden change in tone.

'What?' he said.

'The reason you sent for me. It wasn't really for S&M play, right?'

146

He was aware of his own face freezing in an oddly lopsided expression. Chiaki noticed it too and thought: He's embarrassed. He's so surprised I guessed his secret he can't even speak.

Why the hell would she say something like that, Kawashima was thinking. Why, after babbling on and on about curry-flavoured cream soup, would she suddenly hint that she's read the notes and knows all? Was she taking pleasure in watching his reaction? How do you enjoy someone's reaction when you know it could result in your own death? Had she told the doctor everything after all? Did the doctor call the cops, and were the cops surveilling them at this very moment?

'About the hospital . . .' His voice was trembling a little.

Chiaki thought: He's embarrassed, so he's trying to change the subject. What a bashful person. He's quiet, and he doesn't like to talk about himself or ask people questions, and he's so shy and bashful that he couldn't find the nerve to approach me, so he pretended to be a client.

'Didn't the doctor say anything?' he asked her.
'About what?'
'You know, how did you get the wound, or—'
'I told him I fell off my bicycle.'
'Your bicycle?'

'Uh-huh. Bicycles nowadays, they have all sorts of attachments and things sticking out all over? A thing to hold your water bottle, gear-shift levers, things like that. I mean, I'm not a cyclist or anything, but I read about this in one of those outdoors magazines? That a lot of people get cuts on their legs when they fall.'

'So you told him you fell off a bicycle.'

'I don't think he believed me, but I guess he didn't care.'

'What do you mean?'

'There were a lot of patients waiting, and he looked really busy, so even though he probably knew it wasn't a bicycle accident because of the other scars, I guess he couldn't be bothered.'

'The other scars?' the man said, and Chiaki showed him the four long stripes on the inside of her left wrist.

'I have a lot more on my leg, too, but you can't see them because of the bandage.'

I should have known, Kawashima thought. She's a chronic suicide case. Why hadn't he seen it sooner? The scars on the wrist were right where the skin wrinkled, and her thigh had been covered with blood – but still, he should have recognised the signs. A chronic case, with a powerful drive to destroy herself. Maybe she *wants* me to kill her, he thought, staring at the scars on her wrist and feeling his heartbeat quicken again. Maybe she's just waiting for me to pull out the knife.

The girl took his hand and stood up. She signalled with her eyes and a tilt of the head that she wanted him to follow, and led him across the room to the semi-double bed in the corner. She sat him down on the edge of the bed, then sat beside him, still holding his hand. Her moist eyes looked down at the scars on her wrist, and the corners of her mouth twisted upwards in a smile.

It must have been such a shock for him, Chiaki thought. She reached over and softly stroked the man's hair. He's not over it yet. And besides, he's super-shy, so I'll have to do the inviting. I need to let him know now, before even making the soup, that it's OK to touch me, and kiss me, and have sex with me if he wants.

She could feel her libido squirming to life somewhere deep inside.

'Isn't there something you want to do to me?' she said. The question made Kawashima dizzy. 'You don't have to be afraid.'

So it's true, he thought. She read the notes and decided she'd found exactly the right person to help her die. That's why she was all over him, clinging to him like a frightened child and luring him to her room, and now that she'd got him here she was just waiting for it to happen. But suicides like to leave a record of the act. For all he knew, there could be a video camera hidden somewhere in the room, taping them. Or she might have contacted a friend, an accomplice, who was training a telephoto lens on those glass doors at this very moment. Which would explain why she hadn't closed the curtains.

'Does it bother you that the curtains are open?' Chiaki said when she saw the man staring at the glass doors. 'I can see why you might want me to close them, but I don't really want to, OK? I like to look at all the tall buildings. See the red lights blinking on top? That's so aeroplanes and things don't crash into them, but don't you think they make the buildings look like they're alive? Like they're breathing or something?'

Glancing from the cluster of skyscrapers in the distance back to the girl's face, Kawashima began to feel a little sick to his stomach. She was wearing a smile, and her liquid eyes shone with the reflection of the bedside lamp. She'll probably die wearing that same goofy simper on her face, he thought with disgust. He could see her covered in blood, ecstatically moaning *More! More!* as he slashed her neck and wrists and belly. He'd be nothing more than a tool for her.

What is with this guy, Chiaki was thinking. She

was doing everything she could to help him relax, and all he did was tense up even more. Just how hard did he plan to make her work? Maybe he'd never even had a woman before. Maybe if I put his hand down there, she thought, he'd be so thrilled that blood would shoot out of his nose. I need to be patient, and lead him along gently. First I'll tell him about my sex drive. Guys always seem to like it when I do that.

'I'm the type of person that when I lose my sex drive? Sometimes? It makes me feel really insecure,' she said. She turned back the corner of the duvet and placed Kawashima's hand on the sheet. 'Feel that. You can tell what it is, right? Silk. I bought these sheets two weeks ago. Run your hand over them. It's nothing like the silk from Korea or Taiwan that you buy in department stores, right? Even cheap silk is smooth to the touch, but this is different. It's like milk or something, only dry. Imagine me lying here, and you looking down at me, and these sheets getting wet with, well, all sorts of stuff. Just think what that could be like. You know, I've never let anyone else even *sleep* on these sheets before.'

Listening to the girl talk and studying her face, Kawashima began to feel a very specific old fear. The fear of feeling manipulated by outside forces. He remembered the terrifying story his mother used to tell him after a beating. He couldn't have been more than four or five the first time, barely old enough to understand the words. But she told him the story many times in the years that followed, whenever her beatings failed to produce the desired tears.

You're a weird kid, she'd say, *and when you get older you'll be a crazy person, a nutcase. I know because I had a classmate like that when I was a girl, and I visited him at the loony-bin once. He was in a narrow little room with no windows, and all he did all day long was stand with his ear pressed against the wall, listening to a voice only he could hear and laughing and crying. When he was in my class, whatever you asked this lunatic to do, he'd do the exact opposite. If you told him to shut up he'd start gibbering like mad, and if you told him to eat he'd clamp his mouth shut and grit his teeth and wouldn't open up for anything. Obstinate and contrary, just like you. Wait and see – someday you'll end up in a little cell with no windows, listening to the voice in the wall like that classmate of mine. He used to twist his neck to one side so he could press his ear against the wall, and finally he got so he couldn't straighten it out and had to walk around with his chin touching his shoulder and only his ear facing forward.*

In later years Kawashima had read up on mental illness. People like the one his mother had described were called schizophrenics. And one of the symptoms of a schizophrenic breakdown was the delusion that someone or something was manipulating you, making you say things or do things against your will.

I didn't plan to kill her, officer. It was beyond my control. The girl started stabbing her own leg, and after that she begged me to kill her. She lay down naked on the bed, and when I planted the knife in her she was very happy and died smiling.

Imagine saying something like that, Kawashima thought. They'd put me in the nuthouse for sure. If anyone's manipulating me, though, it isn't this girl. She's just a servant, a slave. Some random suicidal erotomaniac sent by whoever it is that wants me to go insane. I need her to squeal and weep and plead for her life – and look at her: sitting there with her eyes all misty, smiling like the masque of comedy as she imagines me stabbing her to death. She's wet up to her eyeballs with lust and chatting away as if this were the happiest moment of her life.

'Think about it,' she said, moving his hand. 'First you touch the sheets like this, and then, after that, you touch my skin.' She put his hand on her left thigh, the one without the bandage. 'Nobody's ever done this before.'

And that's the truth, she thought. Nobody else has ever touched these sheets – not Yoshiaki or Yutaka or Atsushi or Hisao or Kazuki or anybody. To be able to enjoy the feel of them and then the feel of my body, that's a very special thing. And basically what I'm telling you, Mister, is that it's OK for you to ejaculate all over my new sheets.

Ejaculate, she thought, and felt her smile drain away. I wonder what sort of face he'll make when he comes. Will it be different from the others? How? *Take it in your mouth*. That's what You-know-who used to say. But why do I have to remember *him* now? He made me take it in my mouth. *We can't have you getting pregnant, Chiaki*. You-know-who would make me take it in my mouth, and then right away the stuff would come out. But this man is different. Isn't he? He helped me in the bathroom, and he waited for me in the cold. That's why I thought I'd do whatever he wanted, let him have his way with me, even lick me down there if he wants to. He licks me, and then I take it in my mouth. Take it in my mouth. Then the stuff comes out. Maybe I'm falling in love. Because even when I bit his finger he didn't do anything but kept whispering softly in my ear, and because he stood out in that freezing cold waiting for me. Falling in love with him. Because he didn't do anything. He didn't do anything. Didn't try to do anything. He's different from You-know-who, completely different. You-know-who. *Take it in your mouth. Take it in your mouth, Chiaki, take it in your mouth. Take it in your mouth.*

The girl still had hold of Kawashima's hand but had stopped sliding it up and down her thigh. She was about to say something, then clenched her jaw and seemed to swallow the words. Peering down at the hand that held his, she untwined her fingers and withdrew it. She raised her fingertips to her upper lip, as if smelling them, and closed her eyes. Her lips moved, and it looked as if she were whispering to her hand. When Kawashima gently removed his own hand from her thigh, she opened her eyes and glared at him.

Chiaki knew she was on the verge of snapping again. Looking down at the thigh the man had just rejected, she felt the rage building. *He's just like all the others after all*, she said to herself. But just like them how? And who did she mean by 'the others'? These questions occurred to her, but she didn't have the energy or will to deal with them now. It was almost as if she could *see* the rage – the one thing without which she couldn't survive, without which she'd be helpless. As if she could see the rage come foaming up the pathways from her fingers and toes to her heart and brain. Why do I need this, though, she asked herself, and tears welled up in her eyes. Why do I need this stupid rage? There were times when, having been slowly stretched to the breaking point, she snapped like a rubber band, and other times, like now, when it happened with no warning at all, as if the rage had been cut loose with a blade.

Something terrible always happens when I get like this, she thought. And when it's all over I'll feel so bad I'll want to die. I hate it. I hate it, but I never have the power to stop it, so it must be something I really need. This rage that makes me want to destroy everything I see – all the people and things, and myself too, burn everything down to the ground. I must need it. But why would a person need something like that? In elementary school that time, alone in the equipment room with the young gym teacher. I lifted my skirt and took his hand and tried to slide it inside my underwear. I thought that was what grown-up men liked, and I wanted to make him happy. But he pulled his hand away. The rage took over and I started screaming as if I'd burst into flames, and the gym teacher reached for my hand, saying, *I see – you just want to be friends with me, don't you?* and I bit his hand until it bled. This man too, Chiaki thought and glared at him again. I know he's going to make me angry. Sooner or later he'll do or say *something* to make me lose it. Whether he tries to kiss me or tries to run away or tries to lick me down there or tries to hit me or gets down on his hands and knees and begs for forgiveness, I'll end up in a rage, like I always have, sooner or later, with all the others.

I hate that, she thought, I hate that that always has to happen.

She closed her eyes again, remembering walking along arm in arm with this man, and sitting next to him in the taxi with the lights of the skyscrapers all around. She remembered how cold his arm was to the touch, and the memory cheered her a little. *I wanna do that again*, she thought, silently mouthing the words. *I wanna walk with him like that again.*

'I'll fix the soup,' she declared, and stood up and limped towards the kitchenette. She could feel the man's eyes on her as she walked away from the bed. He's probably really disappointed, she thought. I didn't let him do anything after all, so now he'll be all discouraged. What'll I do if he tells me he's leaving?

The thought frightened her, and she decided to mix some Halcion into his soup.

'I put in too much curry powder, didn't I? Sorry! Was it too spicy?'

No, it was good, Kawashima told her, wiping his mouth with a napkin. He'd devoured two rolls and finished every drop of the creamy yellow soup. Come to think of it, he hadn't eaten anything since that sandwich at Haneda Airport when he bought the overnight bag. He could feel his body warming from the inside out, melting some of the tension.

Chiaki beamed contentedly at the empty soup bowl and carried it to the sink. She turned on the hot water and took a moment to check the contents of the McCormick's spice bottle in the cupboard. It was still about half-full. The label said THYME, but inside the dark glass was a light-blue powder made of crushed Halcion tablets. The dealer near Shibuya Station had suggested this method of hiding the stuff. She'd mixed the equivalent of about two tablets into the man's soup. The reason she'd added extra curry powder was of course so he wouldn't notice, but Halcion was so bitter that she'd worried he might taste it anyway. The man had wolfed it all down, however, along with two buttered rolls, and never suspected anything. He must've been awfully hungry. He'd eaten in silence, sweat forming on the bridge of his nose.

She had slipped half a teaspoon – about three tablets – into Kazuki's food that other time, but Kazuki used Halcion regularly. She couldn't imagine *this* man being a regular user, though. He'd feel the effect of two tablets within thirty minutes and drop like a tranquillised elephant, dead to the world, within an hour. One tablet would've been enough, really, but a lot of times Halcion stimulated a man's sex drive before knocking him out. She'd imagined the man getting all goopy-eyed and horny on her and thought: If he tried to jump me right now, it would only bring back those awful memories. Once he fell asleep, though, he was all hers. He wouldn't wake up even if you cut off his finger.

Kawashima was tired. Gazing at the girl's back as she washed the bowl, he wondered why her attitude had changed so suddenly. Would she try to entice him again after washing up? Or had the idea of being stabbed to death begun to scare her? She'd really given him the evil eye before getting up to make the soup, though. What had brought that on?

He was tired of racking his brains like this and thought longingly of the bed back in his hotel room in Akasaka. He could call the late-thirties erotic masseuse and put all this behind him. It was one a.m. According to the plan, he should have finished disposing of all the evidence and been back in that room by now. He wondered how it would have felt, and wished he could read through the notes. They were in the bottom of his bag.

The girl was washing the bowl meticulously, using only very hot water – no soap – to scrub off the grease and residue. She'd hold the bowl up to the light as if peering through it, and when she spotted the slightest blemish she'd start all over again. When she finally finished with the bowl, she began the same procedure with the enamel soup pan. Kawashima surveyed the room and noticed that there wasn't so much as a stray scrap of paper lying about. No half-read magazines or newspapers, no open bags of chips or boxes of chocolates, no crumpled-up tissues, no fruit peels. The cosmetics on the dressing table were arranged as precisely as pieces on a chessboard, the little jars and bottles all grouped according to size and shape. The L-shaped sofa and the audio rack were equidistant – to within a centimetre, he would have wagered – from the coffee table that separated them, and neither the audio rack nor the bookcase held anything unrelated to their functions. The shelves weren't cluttered with letters or postcards or pills or wallets or memo pads or business cards or paperclips or coins. All such odds and ends were stashed just outside the kitchenette, in a stack of translucent storage cases. He was seated at the two-person dining table, the blond wood of which was polished to such a shine that he could see himself in its surface. The place was like a real-estate agent's model apartment, he was thinking. Immaculate and lifeless. The only exception was the corner of the bed where they'd been sitting. The duvet was turned back, exposing the wrinkled sheets, and the shadows of the wrinkles formed a pattern of irregular, curving stripes on the lustrous silk. Like the rolling hills of some undiscovered country, or scars of violence on smooth shoulders or breasts. Kawashima recalled the suffocating anxiety he'd experienced sitting there next to the girl and looked away, thinking: It must take a lot of work to keep a room this clean, though.

He was imagining the girl labouring for hours at a time to eradicate every last speck of dust when, suddenly, the room shook with such force that he had to grab the edge of the dining table. He looked around frantically, only to see that nothing had fallen or tipped over and that the girl, drying the soup pan in the kitchenette, seemed to have noticed nothing. Not an earthquake, then, he thought anxiously, rubbing his eyes and shaking his head. He sat still, waiting to see if anything else happened, but nothing did. He was just tired, that was all.

His thoughts drifted back to the notes. If only he could lie in bed and read through them! It occurred to him that he'd already forgotten a lot of what he'd written down, probably because things had taken so many unexpected turns. He knew he'd filled seven pages with small, dense writing, but couldn't remember, for example, what it was he'd written first. He thought it concerned either which type of prostitute he should choose or which hotel, but he wasn't sure. He'd scribbled in a sort of stream of consciousness, without any outline or organisation. If only the girl would go to sleep, he thought. He could read the notes right here.

She'd finished cleaning up and was standing in the kitchenette with her arms crossed, watching him. He noticed her checking the clock and glanced at his wristwatch. Twenty-five minutes had passed since she'd carried his empty bowl away. Watching her silently eyeing him from the kitchenette, he began to wonder how she'd managed to figure out his plan. Which part of the notes had she read? He'd been away from the hotel room for no more than a few minutes – maybe only two or three. How much of his crabbed handwriting could she have deciphered in that time? It would be impossible to understand what the whole thing was about just by reading a page at random. Wouldn't it? And she hadn't exactly been in a lucid state of mind. But somehow she'd figured it all out. She knows things she couldn't have known without reading the notes, he thought. The fact that I was staying at a different hotel. The fact that I hadn't called her for the purpose of S&M play. What else?

There was something else, he was thinking, when another tremor shook the room. Again he grabbed hold of the table. The girl was still standing there with her arms crossed, watching him. She seemed to be smiling. The room trembled once more. Then again. Gravity doubled, or tripled, and he had to hang on to the table or risk collapsing to the floor. What is this? he wondered, and was horrified to find himself being sucked inside something dark and enormous. It was as if a huge, diaphragm-shaped iron shutter were closing before his eyes. If I don't get out of here, he thought, I'll be trapped inside. His mother materialised, smiling, in the shrinking window of light. Or was it the suicide girl? Her voice rang in his ears:

I told you so! Look at you – locked inside a narrow cell with no windows!

'Stop it!' he shouted and tried to stand up, but it was as if he'd been turned to stone.

Didn't I tell you you'd end up sitting all day long with your ear pressed against a wall, listening to some voice only you can hear? With your neck permanently twisted to one side? I always said this would happen to you when you grew up! I told you you'd go insane!

It was Mother, all right. The opening continued to shrink. Soon all the light would be gone. Someone was laughing. No. Not someone. Everyone. A vast sea of people laughing. Or cheering. The roar of a crowd in some great colosseum. Beneath the colosseum, in a windowless little dungeon cell, a thick iron shutter was about to seal him in.

He looked down. It was as if his own unconscious had become visible to him in the form of a rising tide. The waves lapped at his feet, then his ankles, his shins, his knees. A tide of swamp-water, sluggishly awash with vomit and flotsam: long-discarded items, all torn, tattered, rusting, bent, scorched, melted, crushed, cracked, oxidised, rotting, fermenting, festering with bacteria and crammed with every imaginable horror. He was up to his chin in the stuff now, and the fear was coalescing into a giant, repulsive insect that emerged from the swamp to crawl up his face and entangle its legs and feelers in his hair. The legs bristled with prickly thorns, and the feelers ended in sharp points that stung his forehead and scalp. Kawashima let go of the table, reaching up to tear the thing away, and fell. His knees hit the floor. The swamp washed over his head, and he shouted for Yoko at the top of his lungs.

At first Chiaki couldn't make out what the man was mumbling. Those two tablets really did the job, she was thinking – definitely his first time taking Halcion. She'd been unable to suppress a smile when he was trying to maintain his grip on the table, but when he tore at his hair and fell to his knees with a look of utter agony on his face, she found herself sympathising a little. The first time she'd taken Halcion, she too had had an unpleasant experience. A panicky feeling at the ferocious onslaught of sleep. Atsushi or Kazuki, she forgot which, had been with her, and she'd fallen asleep clutching his hand. What was it the man was mumbling, though? Maybe he's calling my name, she thought, listening carefully, but no. It was another woman's name. *Yoko*. The blood turned cold in her veins. She gave a contemptuous little snort, as if to disparage her own emotion, and a shudder ran through her body. And then, just like that, something snapped and rage took over.

Chiaki reached for the kitchen drawer, but used too much force opening it, and it came all the way out. There was a great crash as the contents spilled on to the floor, and another as the drawer itself followed. Squatting down, she fished among the scattered utensils until she came up with a manual can opener. She tested its heft and closed her fist around the handle.

It was as she approached the man, who was grappling with his overturned chair, trying to climb to his feet, that Chiaki remembered why this uncontrollable rage of hers was so necessary. She needed it to contend with all the insults. Insults were the calling cards of hostility. And only violent rage gave her the courage it took to stand up to the hostility all around her. Rage alone could show you the way to action.

'Yoko, Yoko,' the man was mumbling. 'Help me, Yoko.'

Chiaki took aim at his droopy-lidded eyes and slammed the can opener down. *My name isn't Yoko.* She heard the stainless steel meet the bone of the eye socket, a sound like a shovel crunching into frozen earth. The man covered his head and tried to crawl away, but Chiaki followed, sobbing and raining down blows to his shoulders and arms and mouth and cheeks and ears.

The first blow dredged Kawashima up from the swamp of unconsciousness. The shock and the subsequent fierce pain reawakened his deadened senses, and the iron shutter was blasted to bits just before closing completely. He was bathed in a sudden, blinding light that screamed of danger, and he tried to shield his face and head. It was like waking from a long but fitful sleep, and it felt as if all the windows in the apartment had shattered and wind was howling through the room.

He heard the voice quite clearly.

Don't say you're sorry, no matter how much it hurts. If you apologise you'll only be beaten harder. It was the same voice he'd heard by the disposable diaper shelf and again tonight, when looking at the new bandage on the girl's thigh, but to Kawashima it seemed as if he were hearing it for the first time in years. This was the voice, he remembered very distinctly now, that had always protected him as a child. *Don't ask for forgiveness. The attack will be over soon. When you're sure it's over, look in her eyes. If you can do that, it won't be a defeat. You will not have lost if you can look her right in the eyes.*

The moment Chiaki realised she was sobbing, her shoulder and arm succumbed to exhaustion and she found herself gasping for breath. The tears coursing down her cheeks dripped from the tip of her chin to the carpet. She was gazing at a single teardrop that sat like dew on the shaggy strands, when all the strength drained from her body. I used up the rage, she thought as the can opener slipped from her hand to the carpet, I used up all the rage. The man, she noticed now, was peeking out between blood-drenched fingers, watching her. There was something scary about the look in his eye. Was he angry? What if he got up and left? She wondered if she should wrap her arms around him, apologise and beg him to stay, but she wouldn't have had the strength to do that anyway.

The girl was just standing there with her face all contorted and her shoulders and chin jerking with silent sobs. *Look at her*, the voice said. *She's crying. She's afraid. You see? You can let down your guard now – she's crying, and she isn't holding the weapon any more.* Kawashima slowly lowered his hands. The sleeves of his sweatshirt were soaked with blood, and he couldn't see out of his left eye because of all the blood from the gash. The back of his left hand was cut and bleeding as well, but he scarcely felt it. Why was the pain fading away, though, when he hadn't even used the technique? It must be the power of the voice, he thought. The voice that came from somewhere inside his own skin and echoed in his ears. That voice had taught him so many things. He hadn't heard from it much since meeting Yoko, but it had helped him out all through childhood. That voice was the only one he could trust.

Chiaki watched the man lower his arms, thinking how ridiculous he looked. He reminded her of the sloth she'd once seen in a Disney movie. The sloth that fell out of a tree. Sloths spend their lives hanging from branches, the narrator had said, and being on the ground is a serious threat to their safety because their muscles aren't built for it. The sloth was desperately trying to get back to the tree, but its movements were slow and weird and comical: clinging to the ground, awkwardly waggling one arm or leg at a time and hardly making progress at all. This man was exactly like that sloth. His movements were totally primitive and retarded-looking, but Chiaki wasn't able to appreciate the humour right now. The left side of his face was like a half-mask of thick, dark red blood, but it wasn't that; it was the way his right eye was staring at her. No one had ever looked at her that way before. It was an ogling, spacy stare, but one that flickered with sorrow and hatred and defiance. He was trying to get to his feet again. And he was saying something to her in a voice she could barely hear.

'Did you find the ice pick beneath the bathtub? The ice pick. Was it under the tub? You must've looked under the bathtub, right? When you moved?'

She didn't understand what he was talking about, but the look in his eye scared her, and she shook her head.

'I need it now. You didn't look under the bath when you moved?'

She shook her head again.

'That's funny,' Kawashima muttered. The smell of burning tissue was not only deep in his nostrils now but swirling through every cell in his body. Showers of sparks shot out where his senses intersected, but he wasn't aware of them in any objective sense, or of the fever saturating the space between his temples. He was already one with the burnt protein smell and the sparks and the fever. The voice was no longer reverberating inside him, but that was all right. The voice helped me out earlier for the first time in a long time, he was thinking, but I can take it from here.

And now he remembered whose voice that was. It's mine, he thought. It's me as a child. I mean, the voice I created as a child. I knew my own voice would be too weak, too childlike and vulnerable, so I chose the voice of an adult. A generic grown-up, like the man who read the news. But now I'm all grown up myself. I can speak for myself, and act for myself. Look at the woman standing there. See how she fears me. The whole *world* shall learn to fear me.

He remembered feeling this way once before. This time the sensation was even more intense, but the first time was when he'd hit his mother. Seeing her after all those years, he couldn't get over how small she looked. As if she'd shrunk. Like the toy monster they used to sell that expanded in water and shrank when it dried. That was her, all dried up and shrunken. Just to see her like that had been enough for him, but then she had to go and act timid and scared. 'You forgive your mother, don't you?' That's when he hit her, when he saw how scared she was. He couldn't bear it that she was frightened and asking for help. Asking for help is wrong. Because there isn't any such thing as help in this world.

Like the woman standing right here, he thought – scared to death and begging me to help her. I'll have to set her straight. I have to let her know that no matter how much she cries, no one's going to come to her rescue. She says she doesn't know where the ice pick is. So maybe the ice pick *wasn't* under the bathtub all this time. Maybe the police took it away after all, as evidence. The police. Wait a minute.

Weren't the cops supposed to be surveilling this apartment? Ah, well. No matter. Just have to do it over there in the corner, where they can't see us. But what about the ice pick? How can I set this woman straight without the ice pick? I've got to hurry. Before my arms and legs get too heavy. All the pain is gone, though. No pain. Mustn't sleep until I've taught her this lesson. Very important. Wonder if she'll try to run. Have to show her she can't escape. Easy enough.

'Come here a minute,' he said.

Chiaki shook her head again and took half a step back. The man lurched forward and grabbed hold of her arm, squeezing so hard that she screamed – or tried to. All that came out of her parched throat was a raspy, whistling sound, like steam escaping. Breathing heavily, the smell of curry thick on his breath and sweat pouring down his blood-slick face, the man dragged her into the kitchenette, to the counter where the espresso machine sat. He ripped the machine's cord from the socket and used it to bind her wrists together. She tried to break free, but he was much too strong for her and didn't even seem to feel it when she kicked him, though the kicking made her thigh hurt again. He wound the cord around her wrists three or four times, pulling with all his might, and ended by looping it the other way, between her hands and forearms. He secured it all with a tight knot, and her skin turned a colourless, ghostly white where the cord bit into it.

'Just tell yourself,' he said as he crammed a balled-up dishcloth into her mouth, 'it doesn't hurt.' He was slurring his words now. 'Here's the secret. You have to believe. If you even *think* it might hurt, even a little, you won't succeed. You mustn't doubt, for even one second, that all the pain will be gone. Look at me. *Look* at me.'

He yanked on her bound wrists, pulling her so close their noses nearly touched. The wound above his left eye hadn't closed and blood was still leaking from it. The Halcion must be killing the pain, Chiaki thought. The eye remained open even though it was awash with blood. Coated with a red film, it swivelled about as if it had a mind of its own. Searching for something in its own crimson world. Like the eye of a broken android, she thought, in some science-fiction movie. Her wrists hurt, and the dishcloth stuffed in her mouth made it difficult to breathe, but she couldn't stop looking at that eye.

I have to show her there's no need to run away, thought Kawashima. He kept talking but was having trouble enunciating some of the words. Twice he accidentally bit his tongue, and he tried to stimulate sensation in his mouth by running a fingernail over his gums.

'I would never, lie to you, I want you, to look at me, but focus your eyes, somewhere behind me, like one of those, 3-D pictures, do like that, that's the secret, my mother, she put ammonia, on my hand, and one time she said, do you want a tattoo, and she sharpened this pencil, a hard one, 4H or 5H, really sharp, and she stabbed my arms, and legs with it, and she hit me, with a milk bottle, and tied up my ears, and fingers, with string, she didn't care, she'd prise open my eyelids, with her fingers, and bring the tip, of a burning cigarette, or a needle, right up to my eye, it didn't bother her at all, so now, do you understand, the secret?'

Chiaki had no idea what the man was raving about, but as she gazed at his swivelling eyeball her ears were registering words like *ammonia* and *tattoo* and *milk bottle* and *needle*, and when he asked if she understood she nodded. The corner of the dishcloth protruding from her mouth flapped up and down as she did so.

'Now I'm going to, cut your Achilles, your Achilles tendons, so remember, remember to do, like I just told you.'

It was hard to make sense of what he was saying, and Chiaki absently nodded again, but when she saw the man squat down and sift through the forks and spoons and cooking scissors and other utensils scattered on the floor, the words *cut your Achilles tendons* replayed in her mind, and she let out a muffled squeal and struggled to get away. The man was holding on to the cord with one hand, and she managed to rip it from his grasp but in doing so brought the espresso machine crashing to the floor. The impact it made caused her to fall backwards and sit suddenly down beside it.

Where'd my knife go, Kawashima was muttering, when his eye fell on the bag he'd left beside the sofa.

'Hang on, a second, I'll get, my knife.'

When he staggered off towards the sofa, Chiaki tried to yank the cord loose from the espresso machine, which lay on its side bleeding dark brown liquid. It was all she could think of to do, but she succeeded only in tightening the loops around her wrists, which were swollen now and turning purple. She could see the man reflected in the shiny stainless steel surface of the machine. He was rummaging in his bag. Gritting her teeth, she began dragging the machine little by little over the floor, hoping somehow to reach the door, but with each tug the cord bit deeper into her. She was breathing rapidly through her nostrils, and her chest began to hurt. The dishcloth was making her gag, and she tried to spit it out; but it was so tightly packed in her mouth that it wouldn't budge. Somehow she had to make it to the door and kick or pound on it in the hope that someone would respond. She remembered how the man had looked in the bathroom at the hotel, whispering in her ear as she bit his finger, and she imagined him wearing the same bland expression as he sliced through her Achilles tendons. Murdering her with the same poker-face he'd worn waiting for her in the freezing cold.

I've never met a man like this before, she thought. He's not like You-know-who, of course, but he's not like any of the others either. When he says he'll do something, he does it, no matter what. And it isn't just the Halcion talking. Halcion confuses your mind but it doesn't change your personality. This is a totally new type of man.

Urging the machine along a centimetre at a time, grimacing against the pain in her wrists and thigh, she'd managed to drag it out of the kitchenette and on to the carpet when she looked up to see that the man had returned. He was holding a small package wrapped in duct tape. She was still a good two metres from the door, and when she realised she wasn't going to make it the strength drained from her body once again. She collapsed to the carpet, and the man bent down and grabbed hold of her left ankle.

Using his grip on her ankle, Kawashima rotated the girl on to her back and pulled her towards him, then sat heavily down on the toppled espresso machine. It made a loud bang, and she raised her head to look.

The man had her left leg pinned fast between his knees. He was stripping the duct tape from the package but stopped to wipe his bloodied eye with the sleeve of his sweatshirt. Chiaki could scarcely breathe. She let her head sink back to the carpet. The dishcloth was drenched with her saliva, and drool leaked from the corner of her mouth. Staring up at the ceiling and listening to the tearing sound the tape made, she tried to remember what the man had been saying a while ago. *The secret. Just tell yourself it doesn't hurt. Focus your eyes like on a 3-D picture. Believe. Don't doubt you can stop the pain.* Something like that. She stared at the ceiling, trying to do as he'd said; but the ceiling was a depthless field of white, and it didn't seem possible to focus on a spot beyond it.

An irrelevant thought was trying to take shape in her mind – something about the man not being two different people – but she did her best to block it out. She had to concentrate on telling herself that she wasn't going to feel any pain.

The bottoms of this woman's feet are strange-looking, Kawashima was thinking as he stripped the duct tape from the cardboard. Every few seconds he nodded and sleep fluttered through him like a warm breeze. We're almost there, he told himself sternly.

We're about to hear what it sounds like when you cut the Achilles tendons. He looked down at the figure lying supine and motionless on the floor before him and thought: Who *is* this woman, though? Her loose skirt was all up around her ribs now, exposing her purple panties and her white belly rising and falling like surf. He was still staring at that small white tummy, with its wisp of peachfuzz, when he tore the last strip of tape from the package. He reached inside the folded cardboard, and it fell away to reveal a thin, sharply pointed, steel rod. It wasn't the knife after all.

When he saw what it was he held in his right hand, the image of the baby lying in her crib flashed through his mind, and he gave a little cry. The woman raised her head again at the sound, and when she saw the ice pick, her eyes widened with panic. Her muffled scream caused the veins in her neck to bulge, and she shook her head violently. The corner of the white dish-cloth swung languidly back and forth as she did so, and the drool slid down over her jawline and dripped to her neck. Kawashima looked from the ice pick to the woman's stomach, thinking: Guess I'm going to stab another one. He let go of her leg and slid forward to his knees, so that he was straddling her. He brought the tip of the ice pick to a point just below her navel, and the woman held her breath, stilling the creamy rise and fall of her stomach. He gently stroked the peachfuzz with the tip of the ice pick and was about to bear down hard when another warm breeze riffled through him, and he became aware of an enormous shadow penetrating and entering his body. Then came the odour of ammonia. A sharp, high-pitched voice saying, *Don't bother coming back!* The sound of a latch being locked. A blurry silhouette on frosted glass. It's Mother, he thought. She's inside me.

The feeling of oneness with his mother was nauseating. It was as if she'd hijacked his body and held him locked in a tight embrace. He was trying to shout the words, *I hate you!* when he lost consciousness.

11

SANADA CHIAKI MANAGED TO reach the cooking scissors and cut the cord that bound her wrists. She pulled the dishcloth from her mouth and gazed for quite a long while at the man's face. She had no intention of calling the police. It would only mean spending hours and hours – if not days – at the police station. In the man's overnight bag she found a notebook and another tape-wrapped package. Inside the package was a big, dangerous-looking knife. She was tired and her throat and chest and wrists and thigh hurt, but she read the notebook from beginning to end. Even after she'd finished she didn't know if what she'd read was a plan for an actual crime or simply the fantasies of a sick mind. But one thing was sure – the man sleeping over there on the carpet was not some prince who'd worshipped her from afar and come galloping to her rescue. Maybe he was a murderer or maybe he was just some pervert who got off on playing one, but either way she was nothing more to him than a body to rent. She got into bed and buried herself beneath the covers but couldn't sleep. She wasn't afraid the man might awaken – the Halcion would keep him knocked out for hours – but she had a lot on her mind.

She remembered the ice pick pressing against her stomach, and realised that she hadn't felt any fear at all at that moment. Was it because she'd resigned herself to death? Or because she was just too exhausted from the struggle to feel anything? Or had she in fact been curious to see what it would be like to be stabbed by this man?

Staring at the ceiling, telling herself there'd be no pain, while the man sat on the espresso machine wrestling with duct tape, she'd had the strangest thought, a thought that seemed completely irrelevant at the time. The man who'd whispered softly in her ear as she bit his finger and the man who'd waited for her outside the hospital in the freezing cold and the man who'd bound her wrists so tightly and wanted to cut her Achilles tendons, were all the same person. That was the thought that had occurred to her, and she let it sink in now. You didn't get the sense that this man was two or more different people. And that made him unique. Unlike any other man she'd ever known. He wasn't at all like her father, of course, but he wasn't like Kazuki or Atsushi or Hisao or Yoshiaki or Yutaka either. All of *them* were capable of turning from the ideal man into the very worst sort of man in zero point one seconds. Whenever the dark side of a man revealed itself, it always felt to Chiaki as if he'd turned into someone else entirely, and only sex seemed to help counter-act the disillusionment and despair. Which was one reason losing her sex drive always made her so anxious.

Telling herself it was to help her sleep, she cast her mind back to when she and the man had walked along arm in arm, and to when they'd been in the taxi surrounded by the lighted windows of high-rise buildings. Never before had she felt so completely saturated with beautiful feelings. That much she was sure of.

Chiaki was awakened by the phone in the early daylight hours. It was from the manager of the club. *Aya-san*, he said through the answering machine, *be sure and come by the office today*.

She got out of bed and went to look at the man. He'd been sleeping for over ten hours now, lying on his left side, with his back to the wall. The wound above his left eye was closed, the blood crusty and reddish-black. Draw a chalk line around him, she thought, and he could pass for a murder victim. She put away the cooking scissors and other utensils that littered the floor, and disposed of the severed electrical cord. The blood-caked manual can opener went into the sink to be washed later, along with the dishcloth that had been in her mouth. The espresso machine was pretty much totalled. She wanted to use the vacuum cleaner but didn't because it might wake him. There were blood and coffee stains on the carpet. She'd have to have it cleaned.

The man's wallet was lying next to the espresso machine. His name was Kawashima Masayuki. She found a snapshot behind his driver's licence. A photo of him and a woman with glasses holding a newborn baby. So that's Yoko, she thought. The woman with the glasses was smiling, but Kawashima Masayuki had no expression at all except for a stern wrinkle in his brow. Peering at the photo, she was glad he was just a client, just a one-night stand. If I saw this picture after walking arm in arm with him two or three more times I'd probably burn it, she thought; ten times and I'd probably hunt this woman down and kill her. Softly opening the refrigerator, she took out a bottle of Vittel and had some aspirin and Alka-Seltzer. She picked up the ice pick he'd flung to the carpet near the entryway just before passing out and placed it, along with the wallet, the knife, and the notebook, on top of his overnight bag.

Sanada Chiaki poured two centimetres of isopropyl alcohol into one of the Wedgwood soup bowls and submerged the fourteen-gauge needle and the ball-closure ring. She washed her left nipple thoroughly with antibacterial soap and snapped her hands into a pair of surgical gloves.

It was while thinking about what would happen when the man awoke that she'd decided to pierce her other nipple. She was sure he'd go back to where the woman with the glasses was waiting. You could hit him with a can opener again or threaten to report him to the police, she thought, but if this man decides he wants to go home he'll go home.

Chiaki believed that if you chose something painful, accepted the pain and left something beautiful behind on your body as a result, you got stronger. She had to get at least a little stronger than she was right now, or she wouldn't be able to bear the loneliness she'd feel when Kawashima Masayuki left. Sitting at her dressing table, she shook drops of undiluted medicinal mouthwash into a ball of absorbent cotton, and used it to sterilise her nipple. She made two small marks on either side of the nipple with a felt-tip pen, checking in the mirror to make sure the line between them was perfectly horizontal. She walked back to the sofa and sat down, then took the needle from the soup bowl and gazed at the tip of it. It was shaped exactly like a hypodermic, only this needle didn't go down into you but through you, opening a tiny tunnel between the cells. She picked up the small tube of teramycin ointment and squeezed about four centimetres on to the rim of the soup bowl. She was coating the tip of the needle with the ointment, when she noticed that the man had sat up and was watching her.

Kawashima had awoken feeling as if the left half of his face were on fire, and for a while he was unable to see anything at all. As his vision and mind gradually cleared, he remembered little by little the events of the night before. He sat up slowly just as the girl, naked from the waist up and wearing surgical gloves, was settling back down on the sofa. Now her attention was riveted on her own nipple. She pinched it between the fingertips of her left hand, holding a sharp and very slender metallic object in her right. Images from the night before were still flashing through his mind. So I didn't stab her after all, he thought. His bag was right next to the sofa, where he'd left it. His coat lay folded on top of it, and on top of the coat were the ice pick, the knife, and his wallet. As soon as I get out of here, he thought, I'll throw the knife and ice pick away. No need to dispose of the notes. Writing them had been exciting. There was something in those notes, something mysterious and vital. Which was why he'd been so obsessed with the question of whether or not she'd read them.

After meeting Kawashima Masayuki's gaze for some moments, Chiaki looked back down at her nipple. She held it steady with her gloved left thumb and slowly eased the needle through. When she pulled her thumb away, it looked as if the nipple had sprouted a silver thorn on either side.

'What are you doing?' Kawashima asked quietly.

'Piercing,' she replied without taking her eyes off her work.

FOR THE BEST IN PAPERBACKS, LOOK FOR THE 🐧

In every corner of the world, on every subject under the sun, Penguin represents quality and variety—the very best in publishing today.

For complete information about books available from Penguin—including Penguin Classics and Puffins—and how to order them, write to us at the appropriate address below. Please note that for copyright reasons the selection of books varies from country to country.

In the United States: Please write to *Penguin Group (USA), P.O. Box 12289 Dept. B, Newark, New Jersey 07101-5289* or call 1-800-788-6262.

In the United Kingdom: Please write to *Dept. EP, Penguin Books Ltd, Bath Road, Harmondsworth, West Drayton, Middlesex UB7 0DA.*

In Canada: Please write to *Penguin Books Canada Ltd, 90 Eglinton Avenue East, Suite 700, Toronto, Ontario M4P 2Y3.*

In Australia: Please write to *Penguin Books Australia Ltd, P.O. Box 257, Ringwood, Victoria 3134.*

In New Zealand: Please write to *Penguin Books (NZ) Ltd, Private Bag 102902, North Shore Mail Centre, Auckland 10.*

In India: Please write to *Penguin Books India Pvt Ltd, 11 Panchsheel Shopping Centre, Panchsheel Park, New Delhi 110 017.*

In the Netherlands: Please write to *Penguin Books Netherlands bv, Postbus 3507, NL-1001 AH Amsterdam.*

In Germany: Please write to *Penguin Books Deutschland GmbH, Metzlerstrasse 26, 60594 Frankfurt am Main.*

In Spain: Please write to *Penguin Books S. A., Bravo Murillo 19, 1° B, 28015 Madrid.*

In Italy: Please write to *Penguin Italia s.r.l., Via Benedetto Croce 2, 20094 Corsico, Milano.*

In France: Please write to *Penguin France, Le Carré Wilson, 62 rue Benjamin Baillaud, 31500 Toulouse.*

In Japan: Please write to *Penguin Books Japan Ltd, Kaneko Building, 2-3-25 Koraku, Bunkyo-Ku, Tokyo 112.*

In South Africa: Please write to *Penguin Books South Africa (Pty) Ltd, Private Bag X14, Parkview, 2122 Johannesburg.*